This book belongs to

_____

Children's
POOLBEG

First Published 1990 by
Poolbeg Press Ltd.
Knocksedan House,
Swords, Co Dublin, Ireland.

ISBN 1 85371 071 1

Cover design by Judith O'Dwyer
Printed by the Guernsey Press Ltd.,
Vale, Guernsey, Channel Islands.

BUGSY GOES TO
CORK

BUGSY GOES TO
CORK

CAROLYN SWIFT

POOLBEG

Rhyme for Mummers

Here be Tenant Blunt
With work for the people,
Saving the theatre
And Shandon Steeple.

Here be Powder Mills,
A landmark worth keeping,
Stay wide awake
Or else be caught sleeping.

Here be Ballincollig's
Old ruined castle,
There's no escaping
From family hassle.

Here be RTE
With cameras and trouble,
Once there is fighting
The trouble's double.

With thanks to Mike Blair and Máire O'Neill, without whose help I would never have been able to visit the farm at Carrigrohane and Ballincollig Castle, and to Niall McCullough and Valerie Mulvin, who first told me about the Gunpowder Mills at Ballincollig.

Contents

1
Here Be Tenant Blunt

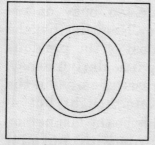n their first morning in Cork, Kate Masterson woke early. The sun's rays were already slanting into her attic room and creeping along the wall towards the little framed picture of St Theresa. The heat wave that had begun before they left Limerick seemed to be holding up. Kate couldn't help being glad, though she knew her father and mother wouldn't be.

She jumped out of bed and looked through the high dormer window across the width of Western Road and the high railings opposite to where the long grassy bank swept up towards the majestic Gothic buildings of University College. She was glad her mother had chosen digs on the edge of the city and not in one of the old narrow streets they had driven through on their way from Limerick the day before.

Now that Bobby's ankle was all right again and he could play the part of the Stableboy once more, Kate knew that everything would be like it was before they had opened in Limerick. Everyone would be either too busy or too nervous to want to talk to her. Knowing that she had played his part for most of the previous week would make Bobby particularly uneasy. He had been fine at the dress rehearsal in the Opera House last night, Kate thought, but all the same she would probably be the last person in the world he would want to be with until after the first night. As for her father, it was never a good idea to speak to him before a first night and her mother would be the worst of all. She would be shouting over the telephone all day or scurrying between the Opera House and the offices of the *Cork Examiner* and the *Evening Echo*, checking books and advertising and trying desperately to get extra publicity.

This time they really needed it too. It was always hard to get people to go to the theatre in a heatwave and, on top of that, they had barely arrived before her mother had noticed there were no posters to be seen anywhere. Only when she began searching for them in the theatre did she discover that the two heavy parcels of big red and black posters lying in the scene dock were exactly the same as the ones Kate had glanced at every day in Limerick. They were suppósed to be almost the same. They still should have read:

PATRICK MASTERSON
in
SHANWALLA
by
LADY GREGORY

with the names of the rest of the company printed in very much smaller letters underneath. What they should not have had were the words Belltable Arts Centre and last week's dates overprinted on them.

Maggie Masterson always had the posters for the whole tour printed at the same time, carefully calculating how many would be needed for each city or town. These were then overprinted across the bottom with the name of the right theatre and dates for each. Now it looked as if they had all been overprinted with the Limerick theatre and dates. Because it was a Sunday, she had been unable to contact the printers and Kate knew that she would be busy today getting slips with the Opera House and this week's dates printed on them and getting these pasted across the posters, which she would want to get put all around Cork just as soon as possible. Then she would want to ring Waterford and Wexford and the rest of the places on the tour, to make sure the same thing had not happened there, to say nothing of trying to see they did not have to pay for what was the printers' mistake.

All this meant that her mother would be the very last person she could talk to, so she had been glad when Mrs Barry, who owned the guesthouse, had mentioned that there was a park only round the corner. There might be other young people there she could get talking to. She slipped on her jeans and tee-shirt and went downstairs to the dining-room with the big bay window, where they had had their tea the evening before.

There was a girl of about her own age at the sideboard, pouring milk from a litre carton into a row of small milk jugs. She had long fair hair tied in two plaits, which swung as she turned sharply at the sound of the door opening.

"Hullo," she said to Kate. "D'you want your breakfast now?"

"I don't mind," Kate told her. "D'you work here?"

"I'm Tina Barry," the girl explained. "I'll tell Mammy you're here."

"I'm not in a hurry," Kate said quickly. "I'd rather talk. You weren't here yesterday when we had tea."

"I was at Carrigrohane," Tina said, carrying two of the small milk jugs and setting them down carefully on the tables near the window.

"What's Carrigrohane?" Kate asked.

"It's just outside the city." Tina took two more jugs and set them on the tables in the centre of the room. "My best friend lives there. At Carrig Farm. I go there a lot in the holidays."

"That must be fun," Kate said, but before Tina could answer she was stopped in her tracks by a peremptory shout from outside.

"Christina! What's keeping you?"

Kate recognised the voice immediately. It was self-important, precise and fussy. Of course, Kate thought, Mrs Barry would call her daughter by her full name.

"I must go!" Tina quickly set the last milk jug on the table over against the wall. "Sit anywhere you like," she said to Kate and hurried out by the door in the far corner of the room.

Kate sat herself down at a table by the window and watched the traffic passing on

Western Road. Already it was building up into a steady stream of cars, vans and trucks heading out of the city for Bishopstown, Ballincollig and Macroom.

"Mammy says will you have orange or tomato juice?" Tina said, suddenly reappearing beside her, "and she's afraid we've nothing only cornflakes before the fry."

"I like cornflakes," Kate said, "and could I have orange juice, please?"

"And there's tea and brown soda bread—or do you want toast?"

Kate shook her head. What she really wanted was to talk to Tina, but Tina had gone again as quickly as she had come. Kate guessed that her mother had told her not to be chatting to the guests when there was work to be done.

Maybe when she brings the cornflakes, Kate thought, we'll have a chance to talk, but Tina had barely set the orange juice and cornflakes on the table when Chris strolled in. Normally, Kate would have been delighted to see him. Of all the actors in her father's company, the young Kerry lad was her favourite, but now it meant that Tina had to scurry away again to tell her mother that Chris would have everything going and the stronger the tea the better.

"Have you to go down to the theatre first

thing?" Kate asked, hoping against hope that she might have his company for a while at least, but she was not surprised when he nodded assent.

"I'm afraid so, Bugsy," he answered. "Did you not hear your father saying after the dress last night that we'd need more tack for the harness room?"

"Can't Ned take care of it?" Kate pleaded, for Ned Flynn was the resident Stage Manager at the Opera House and got all the stage furnishings that were too big or unimportant to travel with them.

"He will, of course, but I've to go through the list with him and make sure he knows exactly what's wanting. We need a deal more clutter in the magistrate's office too. And doesn't it only stand to reason we'd need more of everything to dress a stage that's double the size of the Belltable?"

"I suppose so," Kate sighed. As well as acting, Chris was the assistant stage-manager, so there had never been much hope that he would have time to spare before an opening. Jim Dolan, who had been her father's stage manager ever since Kate could remember, would be sure to have plenty for him to do before the curtain went up that night.

"I only hope your mother knew what she was doing, booking a place the size of the Opera House," Chris continued. "It holds an awful lot of people compared with the sort of places we usually play."

When Jim arrived down for breakfast he had a prop list in his hand and even talking to Chris at table became impossible after that. Kate could only look at the elderly couple silently eating their black pudding at the table by the door and the woman reading a book while she sipped her tomato juice at the table against the far wall, and wonder if they were on holiday. Even when her parents came down they were still too busy arguing over the posters to talk to her.

"That's the last order that man will ever get from me," Pat raged, "And after all the business we've given him over the years!"

"He never let us down before," Maggie protested.

"So why now? Are you saying it's your fault?"

"I certainly am not!" Maggie snapped, "but the important thing now is to get slips printed and the posters up. Time enough later to worry about whose fault it was."

But Kate's father went on muttering that a slip-up over the publicity was all they needed just now and was it any wonder the booking was so poor? Given the mood he was in, Kate was glad enough when he hurried off to do the interviews her mother had arranged for him on Cork Local Radio and Radio South.

Bobby was last down, but he only scowled when Kate told him Tina had a friend who lived on a farm. He was not really needed at the theatre that morning, but Kate guessed he would rather hang around there than stay with her. In fact, he had hardly swallowed his second rasher before he dashed after Chris looking for a lift, though he could easily have walked. He didn't even wait to finish the piece of bread on his plate. Since Bobby usually ate everything he could get, by his own standards he was off his food.

Only Chlöe remained upstairs and Kate knew she was unlikely to surface before lunchtime. Kate thought it must be really boring to lie in bed half the day, but when she had asked Chlöe once why she did it, Chlöe had said: "an actress needs her beauty sleep." With all the others gone about their business, Kate was left to amuse herself until it was time to go to the theatre as audience. She finished the piece of bread Bobby had left on his plate while she thought about what she would do. Tina looked into the room then and asked would she like more bread.

"Oh no, I'm finished, thanks," Kate told her, "and the others are all gone."

"Oh great! I can clear so," Tina said. "Mammy told me I could go as soon as I'd the washing-up done."

"I'll give you a hand," said Kate. "It will be quicker with two."

Tina looked at her doubtfully.

"Mammy doesn't like the guests clearing," she said, but then she brightened and added, "only she's gone to the shops now, so she won't have to know, will she?"

"Well, I'm not going to tell her," Kate laughed, starting to collect the plates and stack them one on top of the other.

"I'll get the tray," Tina said.

While they worked, clearing the tables of dirty delf and putting salt, mustard and pepper back on the sideboard, Tina asked Kate why she had not gone with the others.

"I'm not in the play, you see," Kate explained. "They only brought me because I said I wasn't going to stay at Aunt Delia's on my own."

"You're not a theatrical at all, then?" Tina said, disappointed.

"Oh yes, I am now," Kate told her proudly. "I

played the stableboy for five performances in Limerick when Bobby sprained his ankle." And she told Tina how the man with the black moustache had pushed Bobby into the pit at Silvermines.

"It's like something you'd see on the telly!" Tina gasped, as she wiped the crumbs carefully from the table-cloth on to a plate.

"And that's not all," Kate told her. "Only for me he would have drowned in the flooded mineshaft!"

"Will you tell me the whole story?" Tina begged. "It's boring here serving breakfasts and washing-up every day. I never get to have fun like that."

"It wasn't fun when it happened," Kate said, remembering how her heart had pounded with fear as she raced up the hillside to try to reach Bobby ahead of the car. "But I'll tell you the whole story if you'll let me go with you wherever you're going this morning."

"I'm going to Carrigrohane again," Tina told her, "and you can come if you don't mind a carry on the back of my bike, but we'd want to go right away."

"I'm ready," Kate said, and she followed Tina out of the back door to the shed where she kept her bicycle.

As Tina pedalled past the rows of guest houses, talking was difficult over the noise of the traffic, until most of it had either swung left up Victoria Cross Road or northwards towards the bridge over the River Lee. They kept straight on, coming out on to the south bank of the river with parkland alongside it, opposite a big modern glass building. Beside it was a statue of two men staring up at it in such wonder that Kate laughed out loud.

"What's that place?" she shouted to Tina.

"The Lee Fields," Tina called back.

"Not the park," Kate yelled, "the building!"

"That's the County Hall," Tina told her, pulling in closer to the kerb as a lorry thundered by.

They continued some distance along the straight, wide road, passing a turning on their left and a row of cottages on their right, but Tina kept on going until she reached white painted railings on either side of an open gate between big stone gateposts. Beside them was a tiny little house that Kate loved because it was like the toy houses she had painted when she was small. It was blue and white, with a blue board carved in a twisty pattern running all around it just below the roof.

"Is this where your friend lives?" Kate asked,

looking at the blue and white house in delight.

"That's only the gate lodge," Tina said, "but we'll have to walk to the house. The hill's too steep for riding with you on the back."

Kate looked about her with interest as they set off on foot, wheeling the bike between them. There were a few large trees shading the drive and she thought from the little winged cases hanging from the nearest that it might be a sycamore and wished she was better at knowing the names of trees. Beyond the trees on either side were fields, but she could see no sign of a farm.

Then, as they reached the top of the rise, she saw a house. It was not in the least like Aunt Delia's little house on the slopes of Kilmashogue, but then Kate had never considered that keeping goats was farming. Neither was it like the farmhouses in the children's picture books, which were always long and low with sheds and barns and haystacks beside them and chickens picking in the yard. It was a large, solid, two-storey house painted cream and standing all by itself, more like a plainer version of the big houses at the back of terraces in Ranelagh and Rathmines, across the canal from where she lived, than Kate's idea of a farmhouse.

"Where's the farm?" she asked Tina,

bewildered.

"The milking parlour's across the road," she said, "but we can't go there by ourselves. We have to find Fran."

She led the way past the front of the house and around to the side where a door stood wide open. Kate, who never even visited her best friend in Dublin without ringing the bell and, indeed, could not have done so since the door would be shut and locked, was surprised when Tina just leaned her bike against the wall and walked straight in, giving only a token tap on the open door as she did so. Hesitating just behind her, Kate found she was looking over Tina's shoulder straight into a large kitchen.

Unlike the kitchens she was used to, which were small and used only for cooking, this one seemed to be the place where everything happened, for it was bigger than the Mastersons' living-room and kitchen put together and seemed to be full of people and animals. A lean, dark woman stood at the cooker in the far corner with her back to them, stirring a large pot, while a boy knelt on the floor, brushing the tangles from the coat of an elderly spaniel. A girl with fair, short fluffy hair was wiping down the surface of the large wooden table that filled the centre of the room.

Playing around a cardboard box in the near corner, between the dresser and an inner door, were three tortoiseshell kittens and, as they arrived, a collie sprang up from the hearth and rushed over to them, barking and wagging his tail.

"Hullo, Shep!" Tina said, patting him.

At the sound of her voice, the girl at the table straightened and tossed the cloth in her hand into the sink, but the woman at the cooker merely turned her head, smiled and went on stirring, while the boy shouted at the spaniel, which was wriggling in his grasp. Tina must be so much a part of the family, Kate thought, that her appearance was as much taken for granted as if she had only come from the next room.

"This is Kate Masterson," Tina announced to the room at large. "She's staying with us for the week." She stood aside so they could all see Kate in the open doorway.

The woman at the cooker stopped stirring for long enough to say: "You're very welcome, Kate," the boy released the spaniel and said: "Hi!" and the girl came over to them, smiling.

"Kate wants to see around," Tina said to her.

"If you're going over the road, make sure you dip your feet!" her mother said, "and mind you're back here in time for the dinner. You'll all be staying for the dinner, I suppose?"

"Oh no, that would be too much trouble!" Kate exclaimed, thinking what Maggie would say about imposing herself on strangers.

"No trouble," the woman said. "I already put Tina's name in the pot."

"And she always does extra spuds anyway," the boy added.

"Thanks, Mrs Mahony," Tina said. "Come on, Fran. Let's go!"

"Thanks a lot!" Kate said, feeling that Tina was being altogether too casual about it. As she turned to follow the others out, the collie tried to push past her in the doorway.

"Shut the door!" Mrs Mahony called, "or Shep will be out after you and you don't want him with you if you're going over the road."

Fran thrust the dog back as Kate closed the door fast and they set off along the drive.

"This place is huge!" Kate exclaimed. "There's fields and fields!"

"230 acres," Fran told her, "but you'd need that for a big dairy herd like ours. It's one of the biggest in the whole county."

"Tina said the cows were on the other side of the Carrigrohane Road," Kate said in surprise, as they turned right along a fork sloping upward away from the river.

"There's something I want to show you first," Fran answered. "Up at the old farm near the back gate."

"That's the way Fran goes to school, isn't it, Fran?"

Fran nodded. "It's only a mile from our back gate to the school if you go in the side gate off Melbourn Road. I can nearly do it in ten minutes on the bike. I'm always there before Tina."

"That's because there's so much traffic coming out of the city," Tina argued. "The bus gets held up."

Ahead to the left, Kate saw an old wall and the roof of a barn. Then, as they got closer, she saw a small tumbledown house facing a cobbled yard and, beside it, a row of sheds. It was much more like the farmhouses in her old picture books, with a big round bale of straw beside it.

"Does no-one live here anymore?" she asked.

"Not since I can remember," Fran said. "The cowman used live here long ago, but all the workers have modern cottages down on the road now, with electricity and running water and everything."

A soft moo came from a lean-to and Kate went and looked in. "Oh," she cried, "look at the cow with ear-rings!"

Fran laughed. "Those are fly-tags," she said.

Kate looked at the big eyes of the heifer as she stood patiently, flicking her ears against the flies.

"Is that what you wanted to show me?" she asked.

"Better than that!" Tina cried. "Over here, look!"

In the next shed, on a bed of straw, was a little black and white calf.

"Oh isn't she sweet!" Kate cried, holding out her hand.

"He," Fran corrected, as the calf came over and started to suck Kate's fingers.

"He thinks they're teats!" Tina giggled.

"Where's his Mammy?" asked Kate.

"In the river field with the others," Fran said. "He's on milk replacer now."

"What's that?" Kate asked. "It sounds horrible."

"It's only powdered milk and water," Fran laughed. "Anyway, we'll be weaning him next week."

"Just like a baby!" Kate exclaimed.

"Isn't that what he is?" Tina retorted. "A baby bull!"

"You can give him his bottle this evening if you like," Fran told Kate, "but you'll want to hang on to it tight. He's real greedy!"

They went back down the drive and out on to the Carrigrohane Road beside the little blue and white gate lodge. On the opposite side of the road was a group of buildings surrounded by fields in which cows were grazing.

"All black and white like the calf," Kate commented.

"Of course," Fran said, "It's a Friesian herd."

"I see," said Kate, not seeing at all.

"That's the breed of cow, like a spaniel is a breed of dog," Tina said helpfully.

They crossed the road and walked on until they came to a gate. It looked rather forbidding, with a large notice warning people not to enter without first disinfecting their feet, but Fran just pushed the gate open and walked in.

"Is it all right?" Kate asked uneasily. "Your mother said..."

"We just walk through a dip in here," Fran interrupted. "Follow me!" And she led the way to the door immediately in front of them.

"Why do we have to disinfect our feet?" Kate asked.

"To make sure we don't infect the herd, of course," Fran said. "You'd never believe all the diseases cows can get! There's scour and blow-fly and brucellosis and bovine TB, and if there's the least suspicion of anything when they're testing, you can't send the milk to the creameries for ages and ages, and you lose thousands and thousands of pounds. But if brucellosis was confirmed the whole herd would have to be put down."

Inside the door, Kate and Tina played follow-my-leader as Fran stepped carefully with both feet into a pan of disinfectant and out again on the other side. Then she showed them the milking parlour, pointing out the bulk tank and the gate to the collecting yard and everything, but Kate found it hard to understand how everything worked.

"Come back for the milking at five and you can see for yourself," Fran said, but Kate shook her head. "I have to back for my tea by then," she said. "Maggie will want to be at the theatre well before the half."

Fran looked puzzled and Kate realised then that theatre talk was as puzzling for others as she herself found farm talk.

"That means half-an-hour before curtain up," she explained.

"Then you could come over tomorrow and watch the morning milking," Fran suggested. "They start real early but they don't finish till nine. If you want to come before Tina's ready there's buses for Macroom at 7.35 and 8.45 that will let you off at the gate."

"Then I'll come tomorrow," Kate said, "if Maggie doesn't need me for anything."

"Great," Fran said. "Let's go back now. It must be near time for the dinner."

"You never told me how your brother almost drowned in the flooded mine," Tina reminded Kate, as they closed both gates carefully after then. "And you promised you would if I brought you here."

So, as they climbed the hill, Kate told them all about the painting of the Basket Seller and the Caseys and the man Bobby called Halo-Head. Outside the door of the house, when they reached it, stood a large, expensive-looking white car.

"Da's home," Fran said. "Come and meet him, Kate." But as they reached the kitchen door, she fell silent at the sight of the faces inside. Mrs Mahony stood as if stunned, ignoring the rattling of the lid on the big pot on top of the cooker. At the table sat a large man in his shirt sleeves, with a face like a thundercloud.

"What's wrong?" Fran asked.

"Cork County Council has given Tenant Blunt the planning permission they were looking for to build their chemical factory at

Ballincollig," he answered. "Unless we can find some way to stop them we're ruined!"

"But Jim, it's over two miles away!" Mrs Mahony said. "Surely it's too far to affect us here?"

Mr Mahony shook his head gloomily.

"John Hanrahan was a mile and a half from Merck Sharpe and Dohme, but that didn't save him from losing seventy head of cattle and having half his calves born dead or deformed," he said. "The site's directly up river from us, so any water-borne pollution's going to end up right on our doorstep. And its due west, so most of the year the wind will bring us anything that gets into the air as well! I tell you, if we can't stop it, we're facing ruin!"

2
Work for the People

s soon as Chris arrived at the Opera House, he went looking for Ned Flynn. Bobby followed him through the Pass Door and along the narrow passage connecting the foyer at the front of the theatre with the stage.

The stage was already set for Act One and Bobby could see for himself that the harness room looked bare, compared with the cosy, homely look it had had in Limerick. There were the same bridles hanging on the wall, the same easy chair set by the fireside ready for his father to sit in as the Blind Beggar, and the same table in the centre of the stage for Chlöe to spread out her sewing as the wife of the stableman. Yet, on the much larger stage, it seemed poorly-furnished for the harness room of a rich landowner.

"More tack! We need far more tack!" his father had shouted last night and Jim Dolan had nodded and made a note on his pad.

There was no-one to be seen on stage and Chris, muttering, wandered off to see if Ned was somewhere about at the back of the set. The curtain was up and Bobby stood on the front of the stage, looking out across the orchestra pit into the gloom of the unlit auditorium.

It seemed huge after the intimate little Belltable. He looked up at the back of the dress circle and thought that he would have to make sure his one line carried all that way. No-one had complained that he could not be heard when he had played in *Bugsy Malone* at the Olympia Theatre in Dublin, and that was every bit as big as the Opera House, but that had been a musical where you could play out to the audience. The seats had always been full too. Boasting about the great audiences they had was what had first irritated his father.

"Bugsy, Bugsy, Bugsy!" Pat Masterson had shouted angrily. "Are we never to hear about anything else?" And from that day on he had used the name whenever he wanted to put Bobby down.

"If Bugsy there would keep quiet a moment,"

he would say, "I might be able to think!" or "If Bugsy wants to be an actor he'll have to learn to do what his director tells him!"

It was funny the way the name had caught on, till soon the whole company was calling him Bugsy, even when they were being friendly, so that he had been really annoyed to hear Chris calling Kate Bugsy ever since she took over his part in Limerick. It was stupid, he thought, calling Kate Bugsy. After all, she had never played in *Bugsy Malone*.

He was lucky in one way though. When he came on stage in Act Two he would be running in from the stables, calling urgently to the stableman to come at once, so it would be perfectly natural if he shouted a little. Not like his father, who must speak softly to the ghost that only he, blind as he was, could see. But then everyone knew that Pat Masterson could whisper in a voice that would send shivers down the spine of someone sitting at the very back of the highest gallery in the biggest theatre in the whole world.

He became aware of voices coming from the scene dock at the side of the stage and, turning, saw Chris talking to Ned beside the big skip in which the costumes had been packed. Looking on was a boy of about his own age or maybe a year or so older.

"I've seen baskets labelled 'tack' in the harness room of the Ballycullen Stud in the Curragh," Ned was saying, "And a blind man on a galloping horse couldn't tell them apart from this!"

"It would fill the space nicely, mind you," Chris nodded, "but I wouldn't want some horsy gent coming up to the boss after and saying he never yet saw a racing man that kept his tack in a laundry basket!"

"Ah!" said Ned, "but I've an answer for that one. If I could lay my hands on a saddle or two and a pile of old saddle blankets..."

"We could heap them on top," Chris agreed, "and not a man of them could tell to the differ. Now all we need is something for the Up Right corner. Jim Dolan was saying that a barrel of sweet apples is a thing that wouldn't be out of place."

"The barrel's easy got," Ned said. "I know the very place I could pick one up, but you know yourself it's not the cheapest season of the year to be buying apples and Maggie Masterson keeps a tight rein on the cash."

"Wouldn't we only need three or four," Chris pointed out, "if we were to pack the barrel under them full of straw? And they should last out the week. Then you and I could have the eating of them."

"Good so," Ned agreed. "What else have you got on that list of yours?"

Chris took from his pocket the list Jim had given him over breakfast and the two men studied it together in silence. The watching boy looked across at Bobby and grinned.

Bobby grinned back. Encouraged, the boy went over to him and said: "Hi! I'm Joe Flynn."

"And I'm Bobby Masterson."

'I know. I watched you from out front last night."

"I didn't see you out there with Kate and Maggie."

"I was right at the back of the circle. My Dad said yours is touchy about people being in at the dress, but that if I kept quiet what he didn't know wouldn't hurt him!"

"Could you hear me O.K.?"

"Clear as a bell."

"Great! I didn't want to ask my sister to go up there and have a listen."

"Nor would I," Joe declared, "If I had a sister, that is. I've only a brother."

"Older or younger?"

"He left school last year."

"What does he do?"

"Sign on. He was on a Fás scheme doing up the youth club for a while, but that's over now. He's hoping to get a start with Tenant Blunt."

"What's that?"

"A chemical factory the Yanks want to build out at Ballincollig. Everyone says there'll be loads of jobs going once that gets started."

"I wouldn't fancy working for a chemical factory."

"Isn't it a job, same as another? Ben was saying if he didn't get something soon, he'd try his luck in London and the Mammy's up the walls. She'd be made up if he got something so close to home."

"What sort of work would he do in a chemical factory?"

"Whatever's going. They say they'll take on anyone with a bit of cop-on and train them themselves. The Mammy's doing novenas for the factory to get planning permission."

"Isn't it bound to, with the government mad for anything that will cut unemployment?"

"That's what my Dad said, but then some cranks wrote letters to the paper, saying there'd be a bad hum off it. That started every nut in the land screaming about pollution and wanting surveys done and heaven knows what else."

"I suppose if there was a real stink off it you

could hardly blame the neighbours for cribbing."

"There'll be no-one next or near it," Joe argued. "It's where the old Powder Mills were and there's nothing there now only the ruins of the old mill buildings and the dried-up canal bed. The river's real wide there too, with the site between it and the old British Army Exercise Fields, which are only huge. It's grass all the way up to Iniscarra Bridge, where the County Council have opened a park."

"How come you know the place so well?" Bobby asked.

"When I was a kid, my grandfather brought me to see the old mills and explained how everything worked. Besides, it's near the weir. That's the best place for swimming around here. Since the hot weather started we've been out there nearly every day."

"I never swam in a river," Bobby said. "Only the sea or the baths. Isn't it awful muddy?"

"No, it's great! The bank's gravel and you can walk right out along the top of the weir. I might go out there later on today. D'you want to come?"

"I've no togs with me now. I'd have to go back to the digs and collect them."

"What harm! Loads of fellas go in their

underpants."

"I dunno. I've been off the show for a while with a busted ankle and it's a first night. Will you be going tomorrow?

"Sure. Where are you staying?"

"Mrs Barry's on Western Road."

"Couldn't be better. I'll be passing the door. Be at the bus stop on Western Road about ten past ten and look for me on the Ballincollig bus."

"Joe!"

They turned to see Ned Flynn crossing the stage.

"Come on if you're coming!" he said to his son. "I've a pile of things to collect and you may as well give me a hand loading the car."

"Right!" Joe shouted, and pausing only to repeat, "Ten past ten at the bus stop—see you!" he ran after his father in the direction of the stage door.

***

Kate and Tina had not stayed long at the Mahonys' after the dinner. It had been an uneasy meal. Fran's brother Tim had hardly opened his mouth except to put food in it, and even when Mr Mahony was not talking about Tenant Blunt he was going on about the drought.

"I've never known a July like it!" he exclaimed, as he ladled stew on to his plate. "The cows won't be long mowing throught the river field with the length of grass that's on it now. If this keeps up, we may have to open the silage pits, though what we'll do for winter feed I don't know. And as if that's not enough, now we have all this!" And so it was back to Tenant Blunt again.

"I think I'll go over to Leemount and have a word with Jack about it," he told his wife. "We must all get together and appeal the decision right away. I'm not letting what happened in Tipperary happen here. We've got to fight this with everything we've got!"

He pushed his empty plate aside and stood up.

"There's apple pie," Mrs Mahony told him, but he took his jacket from the chair back and headed for the door.

"I'll have it cold for the tea," he said. "I want to catch Jack before he heads off after his dinner. If we're to appeal the decision there's no time to be lost."

The apple pie was massive, but the good had gone out of the day. After they had drunk their tea, Kate thanked Mrs Mahony politely and said she thought they should be going.

"But you wanted to feed the calf," Fran said, following them out to where the bike still leaned against the wall.

"Oh, I do," Kate told her. "But I think maybe your father doesn't really want us around just now."

"Ah, you mustn't mind him," Fran said. "He's not usually like this. He's just upset."

"Small blame to him!" Tina was indignant. "It's a disgrace, so it is! Who do these people think they are? Foreigners coming over here and threatening the livelihoods of people that have been here man and boy for generations!"

Tina sounded so like her mother that Kate could hardly keep from smiling. All the same, it did seem awful. She thought of the little black and white calf and how terrible it would have been had he been born dead or deformed.

"If you come to watch the milking tomorrow, you can feed the calf then," Fran said. "Do come if you can. Tim's no use when there's anything wrong. He just disappears off with the dogs."

It occurred to Kate then that, if a feeling of gloom had been cast over *them*, it must be still worse for Fran.

"Are you sure it's not making work for your mother?" she asked.

"She doesn't mind," Fran said. "If she wants

us to do anything she'll ask quick enough."

"See you tomorrow then," Tina said, and they were off down the drive on the bicycle, with Kate clinging to Tina with one hand and waving goodbye to Fran with the other. As they passed the County Hall, Kate saw people on the opposite side of the road with bathing togs, walking towards the river.

"Can you swim there?" she called out to Tina, for it was only about a mile from the digs and, she thought, if the hot weather continued, she could easily walk that far for a swim.

"Of course," Tina called back. "That's the baths."

"D'you go there a lot?" Kate asked.

"Sometimes," Tina answered, as they stopped at the traffic lights. "But the weir out beyond Ballincollig's better. I'll take you there one day."

The lights turned green and they were back amongst the heavy traffic on Western Road, so Kate did not bother to reply, but, as Tina was putting her bike back into the shed, she returned to the subject.

"Did you say the bathing place was at Ballincollig?"

"You mean, the weir? It's near Iniscarra Bridge, but you get the bus to Ballincollig West.

Why?"

"Wasn't that where Mr Mahony said the chemical factory was to be built?"

"So it was," Tina agreed. "I hope it won't mean we can't go on swimming at the weir. It's brill there."

"I hope Mr Mahony manages to stop them building it," Kate said. "He sounded awful worried."

She said the same thing to Bobby when he came in to his tea.

"Have you nothing better to worry about than that?" he snapped. "Don't you know that farmers are never done complaining? If it wasn't about the factory it would be the weather."

"It's the weather too," Kate told him. "There's not been enough rain to make the grass grow, so he's afraid there may be nothing left for his cattle to eat."

"And if it rained he'd find something else to moan about, like it was too wet to save the hay or the harvest," Bobby argued.

"He's already made silage," Kate pointed out, "and I don't think he has any fields under wheat or oats or barley."

"He'd still find something else to grumble about." Bobby was clearly not going to give up so easily. "Farmers enjoy a good grumble."

He sounded unreasonably annoyed, Kate thought, but she supposed he was just edgy on account of his first night. It was silly arguing with him when he was in that mood, but she could not help adding, "You can't blame anyone for grumbling about a chemical factory that will kill all his cows!"

"It's not going to kill his cows," Bobby said scornfully. "That's all a load of codswallop. You know nothing about it and nor does he. D'you think the County Council would give planning permission for a factory if it wasn't safe? It's that silly talk that stops people building factories that might give people a bit of work when they need it so badly."

Before Kate could think up an answer, Pat Masterson let out such a roar that she was stunned into silence.

"Can you two never stop arguing?" he thundered. "Isn't it bad enough to have to open tonight to a poor house because someone else boobed, without having to listen to the pair of you going on and on about nothing? We all know Bugsy there is an expert on everything, but when Kate starts airing her ignorance it's too much!"

"Sorry, Pat!" Kate muttered automatically.

No matter how often these eruptions took place, they always scared her, just as her father did when he roared like that in *Othello*.

"Just you remember," Pat went on, talking directly to Kate now and using his sinister whispering voice. "We can still pack you off to Aunt Delia's if you're going to be troublesome."

Kate didn't speak for the rest of the meal. The thought of being packed oof ignominiously to Aunt Delia's like a small child, after having taken her place on stage with the others in Limerick, made her go cold with horror. She thought of Aunt Delia's goats, just waiting for a chance to loom up out of the mist at her when she was least expecting them. If she wanted to be of help to Fran, she was going to have to be very, very careful.

3
Saving the Theatre and Shandon Steeple

ate stood beside her mother in the foyer of the Opera House and watched the audience arriving. They were much more dressed-up than the first night audience in Limerick had been, she thought, with lots of women in short evening dresses and men in dark suits or even tuxedos. Bob Fielding, the theatre manager, came over to them, looking very impressive in his dinner jacket.

"There are some people upstairs in the bar that I'd like you to meet," he said to Maggie. "They're all members of our 'Friends of the Opera House' group, who have made generous donations to the theatre. Will you come and talk to them?"

"Of course," Maggie said, and followed Bob up the stairs to the Circle Bar.

Kate brought up the rear. She had not been personally included in the invitation. Perhaps it was because Bob was so tall that he never seemed to look down as far as Kate. Still, she had not actually been excluded either so, rather than remain by herself in the foyer, she followed the others upstairs.

Since the theatre was far from being full, Kate was surprised to find the bar was crowded. It was a large room, running almost the width of the theatre above the foyer, yet it seemed to be full of people. Kate decided that almost everyone she had seen coming in by the swing doors from the street must be there, rather than sitting in a seat in the auditorium.

"We'll be giving a special reception for the Friends of the Opera House in my office during the interval," Bob murmured, as he strolled into the bar. "You'll be there, of course."

It sounded more like an order than a question, Kate thought. In fact, it was almost a royal command, given the regal manner in which Bob seemed to conduct his business. He led them over towards a fair-haired man with a tanned, rather leathery skin, who was standing at the bar waiting while the barman poured his drink.

"Gary," he said casually, "may I introduce

Maggie Masterson, Pat's better half?"

The man turned and smiled a boyish smile that seemed younger than the face which went with it. "Gary Sheridan," he said, formally introducing himself as he shook Maggie's hand. "A very great honour to meet the wife of the illustrious actor."

There was something about his voice and manner that reminded Kate of someone. At first she could not think who it was but, as he continued to speak, she realised that the voice was like the voice of J.R. Ewing and even the face had something of the look of the man she had so often seen on *Dallas*.

"And who have we here?" he continued, flashing a smile at Kate, who was trying to picture him in a cowboy hat and finding it quite easy.

"My daughter Kate," Maggie told him.

"Glad to know you, Kate," Gary Sheridan said. "Are you an actress too?"

Kate, delighted to be noticed, nodded.

"Only I'm not needed in the cast tonight," she explained.

"You can thank Gary here for the fact that we were able to take your show after all," Bob said to Maggie, lifting the conversation away from Kate again. "It's no secret that the Opera House has been going through a bad patch, after losing several of the companies that booked regular seasons, like Irish National Ballet. We were facing the prospect of temporary closure when Gary here made a very generous donation to our sponsorship fund."

"On behalf of Tenant Blunt, of course," Gary interjected quickly.

Kate gasped. So this was the enemy of the Mahonys! She felt a bit of a traitor just being in his company. But how could this man, who had been nice enough not to talk over her head like the others, be planning to ruin the Mahonys and all their neighbours? Was he like J.R. Ewing in character as well as looks?

"You seem to be helping a lot of people in the city," Bob was saying to him. "Tenant Blunt hasn't even arrived in Cork, but already we have them to thank for keeping our theatre open and the Bells of Shandon too!"

"Don't tell me they were in danger!" laughed Maggie. "Aren't they practically the city symbol?"

"Shandon Steeple badly needed cleaning and repairs, that's all," Gary said modestly. "And what better image could I get for Tenant Blunt than as the company that cleaned and restored Shandon? That should scotch this absurd notion that Tenant Blunt is a dirty industry. Even Bob here had fallen for that one until I met him."

"I was worried about river pollution," Bob explained to Maggie. "I've fished the Lee near the Anglers' Rest for years. That's how I first came across Gary. I was part of a deputation of people concerned about pollution, who called on him looking for guarantees that the chemical plant would not affect the fishing. After he had assured me that my fears were groundless, we got chatting, and when he heard about the theatre's financial problems, he offered to help."

Kate stiffened. It was as if a warning bell had suddenly rung inside her head. When someone had written to the papers calling Tenant Blunt a dirty industry, Gary had picked the best-known landmark in Cork city to clean. When Bob had started asking him awkward questions about polluting the river, he had bought him off with a donation to the theatre. He sounded more like J.R. Ewing every minute. The Mahonys were right to be worried. Gary Sheridan might be charming, but he was not to be trusted.

Bob was bringing them over to meet other people now, well-to-do Cork businessmen and their wives, Kate decided, from the way they dressed and spoke. None of them took much notice of her and all any of them seemed to want to do was talk about her father. Kate thought that this must irritate Maggie sometimes, considering it was she who really ran the company.

Then the bell rang to warn everyone in the bar that the play was about to start. Maggie said that she would see them all in Bob's office during the interval and then she and Kate went with the others into the Dress Circle. When they got there, it was reasonably full, especially the centre part near the front, but there was hardly anyone in the Grand Circle behind it.

"This way," Maggie said, leading Kate along the Circle Balcony to seats right on the side, from where they could see the audience as well as they could see the stage. They were not at all good seats for watching the play, because you would get a stiff neck from screwing your head round to the left all the time, but they had both seen it so often it hardly mattered. Besides, Kate guessed that Maggie was more interested in being able to see how many people were sitting downstairs in the stalls as well as upstairs in the circle, and whether they looked as if they were enjoying the play.

There seemed to be more people sitting in the seats in the stalls than there had been pencilled crosses on the plan of the theatre in the box office that Maggie had looked at with such concern when they first arrived. Kate knew this meant that people must have come along without booking and paid for their seats at the door, which was bound to please Maggie, but even so, the theatre was still only about half full.

Kate glanced sideways at Maggie, who was staring straight in front of her at nothing in particular and Kate guessed she was already doing worrying little sums in her head. Then the house lights went down and Kate hung out over the balcony, twisting her head sideways in order to see Pat, sitting by the fire and clutching his mug of tea, his sightless eyes staring at nothing too.

"Aren't you lucky to have such a talented father?" one of the dressed-up ladies cooed at Kate, as she met her in the interval on the stairs leading up from the circle to Bob's office. "When he stretched out his hand to put the mug down and almost missed the edge of the table you'd really believe he was blind!"

Kate smiled politely. It was one of the little tricks Pat used to lend colour to his part, looking straight at the table and still nearly missing it. It was not specially difficult to do, if you rehearsed it a few times, but it always seemed to impress audiences, though Kate felt sure someone who was really visually handicapped would be well able to find the table.

In the manager's office, a lady was handing round drinks on a little tray, but they seemed to be all wine or spirits. Then Gary Sheridan came towards them, holding a glass of coke.

"I thought you might like this," he said to Kate. "It seemed to be more in your line."

Kate, who had begun to feel quite thirsty, took it gratefully and then felt a traitor again.

"How very thoughtful of you!" Maggie exclaimed. "I hope you thanked him, Kate."

"On the contrary," Gary cut in before Kate needed to say anything, "I have to thank both of you for the opportunity to see a most interesting play. It deserves a much bigger audience than it has managed to attract tonight."

"I'm afraid we were late with our publicity," Maggie said, explaining what had happened with the posters.

"Well now, maybe I can be of some assistance," Gary suggested. "If I might have the privilege of meeting your husband afterwards."

"I'm sure Pat would love to meet you,"

Maggie replied, though, as she muttered to Kate on their way back to their seats: "I don't see what he's going to do about building audiences. It's not as if he already had several hundred factory workers here that he could send along!"

Conducting him to the No. 1 dressing-room after the final curtain, however, Kate realised that Maggie still under-estimated Gary Sheridan. Two photographers, from the *Cork Examiner* and the *Evening Echo*, trotted behind them. Kate knew her mother had asked the papers to send photographers. In fact, she had seen one of them before curtain-up, taking the usual pictures of the more attractive girls and expensively-dressed women, which might appear next day on an inside page with captions saying they had been at the play. All the same, she had never before known them to wait around for the end of a show.

It seemed that Gary was flavour of the month in Cork and, wherever he went, photographers needed very little encouragement to follow.

Pat appeared surprised to see them when the little party trooped into his dressing-room, though he was quick to hide the fact. He was sitting with his back to the door, taking off his make-up, and Kate's first glimpse of his face reflected in the mirror was not encouraging, for he was as aware as Maggie that the theatre had been only half-full. The second he saw the cameras, however, his face lit up with the charismatic smile his fans knew so well, and he turned from the mirror, holding out his arms.

"Kate, my darling!" he cried, as if he had not seen her for years, let alone threatened to banish her to Aunt Delia's. "How d'you think it went?"

"Very well, and the audience loved it," Kate said, with the practice of years, carefully kissing the cheek he held out to her. "But I brought Mr Sheridan to meet you."

Managing to look as if he had only just become aware that there was anyone beside Kate in the room, Pat Masterson rose gracefully to his feet and grasped Gary's outstretched hand.

"Welcome to our little world of make-believe," he cried, in the rich musical voice with the deep organ notes for which he was famous. He was at his most theatrical, Kate thought, and knew that meant he was trying to cover up the fact that he was in a particularly bad mood.

"I'm honoured to meet you, sir," Gary said. "May I congratulate you on a truly fine performance?"

Pat flashed another smile at him and the photographers leaped into action. Next morning, there was a photo on the front page of the *Cork Examiner*.

"Mr Gary Sheridan, project manager of Tenant Blunt, whose planning application to site a chemical factory at Ballincollig is being appealed by neighbouring farmers, congratulating Mr Pat Masterson after his performance as the Blind Beggar in Lady Gregory's play *Shanwalla*, which opened a week's run at the Opera House last night," ran the caption. Maggie was delighted.

"That's the sort of publicity you can't buy," she crowed, throwing the paper on to Pat's bed for him to see. "If that doesn't help the bookings nothing will!"

"And what a delightful man!" Pat said, though Kate could not remember Gary saying anything more than people usually said in the circumstances. "It's outrageous that he's getting all this opposition to his plans. It's high time people in this country realised we have to move with the times!"

Kate thought about the things Mr Mahony had said had happened at that other farm, near the chemical factory in Tipperary, but she knew it was no use telling Pat about that.

She had already had her breakfast, impatient as she was to catch an early bus to Carrigrohane, and Maggie had been out early to buy the paper, but Pat was propped up on pillows in bed, wearing a black and gold kimono over his pyjamas. In helping to get him publicity, Kate thought, Gary had certainly gone exactly the right way to please him.

She studied the photo over her father's shoulder. It was a very good photo, but all this talk about Gary Sheridan had meant she would not now be able to catch the 7.35. Still, it would have been very unwise, after what Pat had said to her the day before, not to have shown a proper interest in the publicity and the good review on the inside page.

"Was there something you wanted?" Maggie asked her finally, for it was unlike Kate to come knocking on their bedroom door before Pat was up.

"I was wondering, do you need me for anything this morning?" Kate asked cautiously, glad they both seemed to be in such good humour again.

"No. Why?" Maggie switched her full attention from re-reading the good notice to her daughter. "Where are you off to?"

"Just some people I met yesterday who have

a farm. They're friends of Tina Barry's and they said I could watch the milking and feed the calf."

It sounded a perfect way of keeping Kate out of her father's hair for the day, Maggie thought.

"Is Bobby going with you?" she asked, for her son had not yet put in an appearance.

"Ah no," Kate said. "I think he's doing something with Joe Flynn."

"Who?" Pat managed to stretch the single word out till it sounded like the cue for the line to bring the curtain down on Act One of some farce.

"Ned Flynn's boy." Maggie turned back to Kate. "That's all right then. Are they collecting you?"

"The bus will drop me off at the gate," Kate said, "If I could have some money for the fare."

Pat reached for a pile of small change beside him on the bedside table and scooped up the lot.

"Here," he said with unaccustomed generosity. "Don't spend it all in the one shop!"

"Oh, thanks, Pat! Thanks a lot!" Kate cried, thrusting the money into the pocket of her jeans and running from the room for fear he would change his mind.

He really was in good humour today, she thought, so Gary Sheridan and his photographers had brought luck to her too. All the same, Gary was going to be a dangerous enemy. He had won Pat and Maggie's support as easily as he had done Bob's and that of the people of Cork, who measured their lives by the Bells of Shandon. The Mahonys would need every bit of help they could get.

Even Bobby seemed to be against the farmers, for some reason Kate could not understand, though he had never once mentioned Gary and she did not even know if he had met him. As she stood at the stop on the Western Road, waiting for the 8.45 bus to Macroom, Kate thought again about the little black and white calf and knew whose side she was on.

"I'll have to do whatever I can," she decided, "but it's going to be an awful fight."

4
Here Be Powder Mills

ate saw Fran before the bus had even stopped. She was leaning against the white-painted railings, waiting.

"I knew when you weren't on the 7.35 you'd have to be on this bus if you were going to make it at all," she said, as it disappeared around the bend of the road under the steep cliff-face topped by Carrigrohane Castle. "I wanted to save you having to come up to the house. The milking will be over soon."

"Tina will be here as soon as she's finished with the breakfasts," Kate said, as they hurried across to the gate beside the warning notice. Walking through the disinfectant dip, as she had done the day before, she could hear a strange mix of sounds coming from the milking parlour: the swish of tails, the patter of shifting feet, the chomping of jaws, the occasional moo and the little tic-tic-tic of the stimulator.

When she arrived, she found the cows ranged in a circle, the milk pumping from the clusters into the almost-full recording jars that hung beneath each one.

"Which is the calf's mammy?" Kate asked.

"That's her over there on the far side," said a tall, lean man with dark eyes.

"She must miss him dreadfully," Kate said.

"She made a fuss right enough when he was first taken away," the man said, "but she's over it now."

"Oh, look!" Kate cried suddenly, "She's wearing a necklace!"

The man laughed.

"That's for the transponder disc," he explained. "They all have them, so the computer will know which is which."

When all the milk had flowed from the pipe line through the cooler into the bulk tank, the men removed the clusters from the cows' udders and then suddenly everything started to revolve.

"Oh!" Kate cried, "the cows are on a roundabout!"

Everyone laughed and the man who had answered her before said :

"Aye, we have all the fun of the fair around here!"

As the carousel brought each cow to the point facing the door she ambled out, tail swishing, into the field outside and straight over to one of the ring feeders, where she began munching away as if she had been on a diet for days.

It had been interesting to watch, but it was feeding the calf that Kate had been looking forward to.

"Hold the bottle this way," Fran instructed, as the calf butted against her in his excitement. "Then he can get it easy. And hold it tight," she added as he almost dragged it from Kate's hand.

"He's real greedy!" Kate laughed, looking at the flaring nostrils and the tiny trickle of milk at the corner of his mouth.

"He's growing fast," Fran said. "He'll have to learn to take his feed from a bucket next week."

Going back towards the house, they met Tina toiling up the drive on her bike.

"I brought the togs," she said to Kate, nodding towards the two bundles of towelling in the basket on the front of her bike. "It's so hot I wish I could jump into cold water right up to my neck this minute."

"We're going to go out to the weir for a swim later on," Kate said to Fran.

"Brill!" Fran shouted. "Let's take the bikes. Then we won't have to be waiting on the buses."

"I'm not taking Kate on the carrier again!" Tina declared. "It's too hot and she's too heavy!"

"Tim has to go to the dentist for a filling," Fran said. "We'll get a lend of his bike. Otherwise we'd have to wait for the 11.40 from the back gate."

Mrs Mahony was sitting at the kitchen table making out a shopping list.

"I've to go into town with Tim," she said, "but you can pack yourselves lunch. There's cold ham and tomatoes in the fridge and apples in the basket there. D'you want the thermos?"

"Ah, no," Fran said. "We'll get minerals in Ballincollig."

"Will you now? And what will you use for money?"

Kate put her hand into the pocket of her jeans and brought out the fistful of money Pat had given her. "I'm rich today," she said.

So, half an hour later, Tina, Fran and Kate pedalled past Carrigrohane post office and on up the hill towards the new roundabout, their bathing things strapped to their carriers and the basket on Tina's bike full of apples and rather untidy-looking ham and tomato sand-wiches, wrapped in the paper off yesterday's sliced pan.

They bought minerals at the newsagents in the main street of Ballincollig, before turning right in Ballincollig West and coasting down the hill towards Iniscarra Bridge, where a stocky round tower stood close to the park gates. There were a handful of cars in the new car park, but they saw only one elderly man walking his dog beside the sluice gate that reminded Kate of the lock gates on the Grand Canal near their home in Dublin. Then they rounded the bend and saw the weir in front of them.

There were people there all right, either swimming in the river or paddling on top of the weir. They were mostly women with small children and elderly people sitting on the river bank with their feet in the water, but there were a few young people too, swimming in the natural pool above the weir. The water sparkled like crystal with the sun shining on it and they lost no time in slipping on their togs and into the cool, clear water.

"Oo, it's freezing!" Kate cried, but it was lovely all the same and it was no longer freezing once you had plunged right into it.

The girls were splashing each other with much laughter when Kate suddenly heard a familiar voice.

"Race you to the far side!" it shouted and Kate looked up to see Bobby and Joe Flynn racing towards them, scattering small children in all directions and splashing the old people on the river bank with their kicking.

"What d'you think you're at?" she shouted at Bobby, as he streaked past her to win by a short head.

"You're not swimming in the Olympics, you know," Tina said in her "Mrs Barry" voice. "Those little kids have as much right to enjoy themselves as you do!"

"Of course, you two had to be here!" Bobby cried in disgust. "Did you meet my sister, Joe? Kate Killjoy, who likes to complain about fellas enjoying themselves and chemical factories getting built!"

"Don't tell me, Kate, that your brother *wants* Tenant Blunt to build a smelly old chemical factory around here?" Tina remarked, nose in air.

"As a matter of fact, I do," Bobby said, "and so does Joe, don't you Joe?"

"And there's plenty more besides my brother hoping to get work out of it," Joe added angrily.

"And there's plenty besides my father that could be ruined by it!" Fran shouted, equally angrily.

For a moment the boys and girls stood confronting each other in the river. Then Kate broke the tension.

"This is crazy," she said. "We came here to enjoy ourselves, not to fight."

"O.K." Joe agreed. "I'll race the lot of you to that tree."

There were no other bathers up river away from the weir, in the direction in which he was pointing.

"Right," Kate shouted: "Are you ready? Steady—go!"

Bobby won again and his victory immediately put him in good humour.

He was like Pat in that, Kate thought to herself. It was funny the way Tina could suddenly remind her of her mother and Bobby of his father.

"Hey, Bobby!" she called. "D'you think I'm like Maggie?"

"Of course not, ya eejit!" he shouted back. "You're not even good at maths!"

All the same, he was laughing as he said it and there was no more arguing until they had all changed out of their wet togs and the girls sat down on the river bank to eat their packed lunch.

"Give us an apple!" Bobby coaxed.

"I will not!" Kate said. "Eat your own lunch!" The boys looked at her in silence.

"I don't believe they brought any," Fran said.

"Isn't that typical?" Tina commented smugly. "Boys never think!"

"Here!" Fran threw an apple at Bobby. "Catch!"

"Good girl yourself!" Bobby shouted gleefully, as he caught it and sank his teeth deep into it. "Mmm! Deadly!"

"That's not fair!" Kate cried. "Why should he eat yours?"

"Because you're too mean to give me yours!" Bobby said with his mouth full.

"That's O.K. I brought two," Fran said, "And anyway I've got my sandwich."

"We all have," Tina pointed out, "But I'm going to eat all mine because I'm hungry. It's not my fault they hadn't the wit to bring anything themselves!"

"And I bet you still have your first communion money!" Joe said. Then he looked hopefully at Kate.

"Oh, alright!" Kate said. "Anything to shut you up!"

"Thanks!" Joe took the apple from her and polished it on his shirt sleeve. "I'm sorry I

shouted at you about Tenant Blunt, but Ben's
counting on it for a job and the Mammy's going
spare for fear all these protests will prevent the
factory from opening."

"And Fran's Da's going spare for fear they
won't!" Kate pointed out. "Couldn't your
brother get some other job that won't kill Mr
Mahony's cows?"

"There aren't any other jobs," Joe retorted.
"And Mr Mahony can forget about his old cows
because the factory's not going to cause
pollution. Mr Sheridan's said that till he's blue
in the face."

"That's all lies!" Fran protested. "My father
says Merck Sharpe and Dohme promised the
same thing when they were looking for
planning permission, but they weren't even in
full production when the cows and sheep for
miles around starting getting streaming eyes
and breathing problems."

"Tenant Blunt's different!" Joe argued.
"They're doing an environmental impact study.
And they're going to have their incinerator
completely enclosed and keep monitoring
everything that comes out of it, to make sure
there's no air pollution."

But Fran was not convinced.

"And I suppose if they find out there is they're

going to tell everybody!" she said. "My father says it's the County Council that should be doing the monitoring and anyway, even if there's no air pollution, they'll be discharging effluent into the river that will wash straight down to our farm."

"Yes, but it won't do any harm to your cows. It won't even harm the fish!" Joe was getting indignant. "Mr Fielding fishes near the Anglers' Rest and he told my father Tenant Blunt did a survey and proved the effluent won't pollute the river."

"And suppose they have an accident?" Tina countered. "Anyway, my father says he wouldn't believe the gospel out of that Gary Sheridan's mouth!"

"That's just silly prejudice!" Bobby said. "My father thinks he's the greatest."

"Because he conned him, the way he conned Bobby Fielding," Kate shouted. "Of course Bob Fielding's going to say whatever Gary Sheridan wants him to say. He bribed him with money to keep the Opera House open! Bob has to back Tenant Blunt now!"

"Well, my father doesn't!" Fran was shouting defiantly now. "He's getting all the farmers to join together to appeal against the decision to grant planning permission."

They were all at it again, Kate thought, lined up in two camps, boys against girls.

"Where exactly do they want to build the factory?" she asked suddenly. "It won't stop people swimming here, will it?"

"Of course not," scoffed Joe. "It's way downstream from here, where the old powder mills were."

"I didn't know they made powder in mills," Kate said in surprise.

"Not face powder, ya eejit!" Bobby roared. "Gunpowder!"

Kate's eyes widened. "You mean, for blowing up things?"

"For firing cannons," Joe told her. "In the days of Napoleon, when Britain was at war with France. Of course, Ireland was under British rule then, so the British Army bought the mills and built the barracks specially to protect them."

"The barracks is inside that big high wall we passed," Fran explained. "The one running almost all the way along one side of the main street of Ballincollig. The Irish Army has it now."

"So how can they build a chemical factory inside the barracks?" Kate asked.

"It's not in it, it's behind it," Joe explained.

"You can get there along the river from here. And you can still see the old mills and workshops and everything. My grandfather remembers when they were still working. He said that in his father's time there were 500 people employed there."

"I'd like to see the mills," Bobby said. "Could you still make gunpowder in them?"

"Not at all," Joe said. "They're only ruins now."

"All the same, I'd like to see them," Bobby persisted.

"We could walk back that way," Joe told him, "if you liked. But there are a few buildings near here. They built them away from the others for safety. My grandfather said they used keep watch all the time from the round tower down by the gate, for fear of explosions. There's one of the mills back there."

They all turned to see where he was pointing.

"D'you mean that thing like a tumbledown stone shed?" Bobby asked.

"That was the old corning mill, Grandda said," Joe explained, "where the mixture was ground down into powder. Then it was sent for drying and glazing and packing into barrels."

"And can you still see where they made the barrels?" Kate asked.

"At the moment you can," Joe said. "The cooperage and saw mills are near the saltpetre refinery and the place where the charcoal was burned. But I suppose they'll all be bulldozed when they build the chemical factory."

"Then we ought to go and see them now, while they're still there," Kate suggested. "They sound interesting."

"I don't see what's interesting about a lot of old ruins," Tina grumbled. "Not if they're all like that old wreck over there..." but Kate gripped her arm.

"I want to see where they plan to build the chemical factory," she whispered, "only I'm not saying that to them!"

Fran nodded quickly.

"We can wheel the bikes along the river path," she said. "There's a road from there up through the East Gate."

"I suppose you can come too," Bobby said grudgingly, "seeing that you gave me your apple!"

"We don't need your permission," Tina began. "It's a free country..."

But Kate gave her a wink and she let her voice trail away. Then all five set off downstream along the south bank of the River Lee.

As they went, Joe pointed out parts of the old mill complex, like the Press House, where they used to press the mill cakes to remove the water that the workmen had poured over them on the way there, to make sure they would not explode the minute they were mixed, and the magazine where the barrels full of gunpowder were stored.

They had walked quite a distance when suddenly the broad paths and neatly-trimmed borders came to an end and they had to manoeuvre the bikes over a rough track right beside the river. It seemed wider than at the weir, so that the cluster of four or five large houses with gardens running down to the far river bank looked as if they were on the other side of a big lake.

"This is where most of the mill buildings were," Joe said, leading them away from the river over rough ground into what looked like a large field that had run wild.

Kate looked around her, expecting to see mills on every side but, at first, she could only find one or two. Then she saw bits of grey wall in amongst a clump of trees here and a bush there and realised that ivy, grass, weeds and leaves had grown over most of what was left of the old Powder Mills.

"This was the Charcoal Burning House," said Joe, pointing to the remains of a square building close to where they stood.

"What *is* charcoal?" asked Tina, more interested than she had expected to be.

"It was made from burning the wood from alder trees," Joe explained, and Kate found herself wishing for the second time in two days that she knew the names of the different trees.

"How can you tell which are the alders?" she asked.

"You'll find a good few around here," Joe told her, "because they needed lots of them and they grow well on marshy ground. There's one over there."

"Where?" Kate asked.

"There! The one with the single fork close to the ground. It's dark wood."

"Like ebony?" Tina asked, but Joe shook his head.

"Not as dark as ebony, but that doesn't grow in Ireland. I think it comes from Africa or somewhere."

"I wish we could see the mills the way they were," Bobby said, inspecting what could still be seen of the charcoal burning house.

"Or even the way it is now," Kate added, "if someone just cut back all the grass and weeds and ivy the way they have in the park, so you could see enough of the old buildings to picture how they were."

"Why bother their heads when it's all about to be knocked?" Joe shrugged.

"Don't bet on that!" Fran shouted. "If my father has anything to do with it, there'll be no chemical factory!"

"Can you kids not read?"

The angry shout came from behind them and they turned to see a fat man with little piggy-eyes and a red face coming towards them from the far corner of the field, where the roofs of several houses could be seen.

"'Course we can! Why? What's it to you?" Bobby demanded rudely.

"Then I'm going to report you for disobeying the notice!" he stormed, the sweat breaking out on his forehead.

"What notice?" Kate was genuinely puzzled.

"Don't pretend you don't know. That act won't wash with me. The notice on the gate, what else?"

"We came through from the park," Joe told him, "along the river. We didn't come in by the gate."

"Well, if you had, you would have seen the notice," the man said, mopping his brow. "It says: 'No admittance. Trespassers will be prosecuted!' "

"Well we didn't see the notice," Tina said pertly, "so it's not our fault. We couldn't read something we didn't see, could we?"

"Don't give me cheek! I'll have barbed wire up along the edge of the park by next week and if I ever see any of you kids in here again, you'll be sorry! D'you hear me now? Stay away from here or I won't be responsible for what happens to you!"

5
A Landmark Worth Keeping

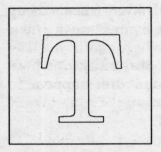here seemed to be nothing to do except leave and Joe led the way across the field in the direction from which the man had come.

"That's the saltpetre refinery," he said, as they passed the remains of a long building close to the mill race.

They all made a great show of inspecting it, in order to prove that they were going in their own good time, but a roar from behind them made them quicken their pace. Though Joe told them that the cluster of ruined buildings beyond the gap in the ditch was the cooperage, where the barrels were made, and opposite them the sawmill where they used to cut the wood for the barrels, with the charcoal mills on the far side, they only gave them a hurried glance.

"I can't see what harm we were doing," Kate muttered.

"Piggy-Eyes must be something to do with the chemical factory," Bobby pointed out.

"And he probably heard what I said about stopping the factory from being built," Fran whispered.

"So what if he did?" Tina was indignant. "We weren't stopping it by being there, were we?"

"Unless there was something he didn't want us to see," Kate suggested.

"But there was nothing there," Joe said. "It was the same as it's been for ages. He was just angry at us being there when we weren't supposed to be. They must have put up the notice since I was there last."

"They probably put it up when Tenant Blunt bought the site," Fran said. "There it is, look!"

They were on a proper track now, heading from the gap in the ditch towards the back of a row of houses that stood behind the remains of the cooperage. In front of them was a closed gate and on it a notice facing away from them. The gate appeared to be locked but, when Joe gave it a sharp tug, it opened.

"If they don't want people coming in they should keep it locked," Tina said, sounding like her mother again.

"Maybe it's only open because your man's there," Bobby said, as they all trooped through on to the road.

Joe closed the gate behind them and they all turned to read the notice.

"He was right about that, anyway," Kate said.

"Of course he was," Joe said. "He should know. He's the builder. Look there!"

They saw then that there was a white van parked outside the gate.

On its side was written, in large black letters:

LEESIDE CONSTRUCTION, LTD.
DEVELOPERS AND BUILDING
CONTRACTORS
INDUSTRIAL—DOMESTIC—
COMMERCIAL
PLANT HIRE—DEMOLITION—SITE
DEVELOPMENT

"Demolition!" echoed Bobby. "Piggy-Eyes has the contract to knock the old Powder Mills!"

"We've just got to stop him! We've *got* to!" Fran declared, her teeth clenched in determination.

"Speak for yourself!" Joe said. "What are they

only ruins? Once they gave work to five hundred people. Now they're old and good for nothing. A chemical factory will give work the way they used do."

"They might be good for something," Kate argued. "What about the tourists? There's people coming from all over the world to see the Rock of Cashel, just *because* it's so old!"

"The Rock of Cashel was built in eleven hundred and something," Bobby scoffed. "When were the mills built, Joe?"

"Near the end of the seventeen hundreds, I think."

"That's pretty old," Kate said. "Two hundred years."

"It won't bring the coach tours," Bobby retorted.

"Maybe they thought that about Cashel when it was only two hundred years old!" Tina said.

"Except that they didn't have coach tours in the thirteen hundreds," Bobby said in his most putting down voice.

"And even if the tourists came," Joe added, "who's going to make money out of it? Coach tour operators, shopkeepers, caterers and the people who write and sell guide books—not people like Ben."

"Wouldn't they all have to take on extra workers?" Kate asked hopefully.

"Not like a big multi-national," Bobby told her. "We can't live in the past. I bet when the people that first built the mills came here there were other people against them!"

"Of course," Fran cried. "The people that grazed cattle here or grew crops. Because it was their living they were losing, the way my father would be losing his. The chemical factory's got to be stopped and I'm going to do my best to stop it!"

"Me too!" shouted Kate. "Come on, let's go!" And she swung her leg over the bar of Tim's bike and rode furiously away from the gate, followed by Fran and Tina, leaving the two boys looking after them.

"Wouldn't it give you the sick?" Joe burst out.

"Don't mind them," Bobby said. "What can they do? They're only girls!"

"Oh it's not them. It's the father. I wouldn't say even he'd be able to stop the factory going ahead in the heel of the hunt, but an appeal's going to delay everything. If it gets put off for too long, Ben will be gone. He's not the sort to hang about. He's already fed up to the teeth with signing on."

"It would give you the sick all right," Bobby

agreed, but his attention was on the van. It was six feet high, but it was longer and smarter than the Land Rovers and Land Cruisers he had seen used as vans. He walked around to the front to read the name of the make on the bonnet.

"A Range Rover," he commented.

Joe nodded. "Four wheel drive and good over bumpy ground. Just the job for a builder. You could drive it on to any site."

"I didn't know they did a commercial version," Bobby said.

"You don't see too many about," Joe agreed. "They're too pricy for most builders. Piggy-Eyes can't be short of the readies."

"Looks as if it holds a fair bit of equipment too," Bobby said.

He peered in the passenger side window, but there was plywood stacked behind the front seats so it was impossible to see into the back. He walked around to the rear of the car to look in through the back window.

"He's got that stuff pasted over it," he said to Joe in disgust. "The sort that lets you see out but stops people seeing in! He must have a lot of expensive gear in it."

"Maybe he just doesn't like people gawking in," Joe said. "You heard how he went on just now. And, by the same token, we'd better split.

He won't take too kindly to you casing his van!"

Reluctantly, Bobby followed him as Joe led the way back to get the bus. As for Joe, he would have been even more worried if he had known what the girls were planning.

Having cycled away from the others at top speed, Kate had slowed as she reached the end of the straight, tree-lined stretch of road, waiting for Fran and Tina to catch up with her.

"Which way?" she asked.

"Straight on up the hill," Fran told her. "The road to the left only goes to the Long and Short Ranges."

"Are they for shooting?" Kate asked. "I suppose the barracks would have had a shooting range."

Angry though she was, Fran started to laugh.

"Not at all," she said. "They're cottages. I think they were where the millworkers lived. I don't know why they called them that though. Maybe there was a rifle range once."

"I wouldn't care to be living there after the chemical factory's built," Tina puffed, as they toiled on up the hill. "If there was a hum off it they'd be right in the firing line then all right."

"It would be even worse for the houses near the gate into the Powder Mills," Fran said.

"They'll be right on top of it."

"Hey!" Kate called. "I've an idea!"

They had reached a bend in the road where the hill was even steeper and all three dismounted.

"How many cottages are there in the Long and Short Ranges?"

Fran thought for a minute as they pushed their bikes up the last stretch of hill towards the stone pillars of the great East Gate of the barracks, which gave on to the main street of Ballincollig.

"Maybe twenty," she said.

"With four or five people in each of them?"

"Less," Fran told her. "A lot of them have old people living on their own or an old couple."

"But there could be thirty or forty people living there anyway?"

"I suppose so. Why?"

"And another five or six houses near the mill gate, with one or two people in all of them?"

"More," Fran said. "One of them's a nursing home. There could be more than twenty people in it."

"Great!" Kate said. "Then that's what we can do. We can write a letter and get them all to sign it, like the Anti-Blood Sport people did."

"What would we say?" asked Tina.

"Something like...wait now...we could say: We, the undersigned object to a chemical factory on the site of the old Powder Mills at Ballincollig. And then we can go round to all the houses getting people to sign it."

"That's brill!" Fran cried. "But I think we should go to houses in Ballincollig too. I mean, they might take more notice if there were hundreds and hundreds of signatures."

"But what would we do with all the signatures when we had them?" Tina wanted to know.

"Show them to the planning people, maybe," Kate said. "Or even the Taoiseach. Fran's father would know, wouldn't he?"

"Of course, he would," Fran cried. "Oh, Kate, you are clever! And if we get loads and loads of signatures they can't say it's only the farmers complaining again!"

At Mrs Barry's next morning, Kate found the good humour that had warmed the house like sunshine the day before had gone. Good notices and publicity had been slow to take effect and bookings at the Opera House had not yet picked up.

"It's the weather," Kate said. "No-one wants to be indoors when it's as hot as it was yesterday evening. They were all by the river. I saw them all coming home."

"The age-old excuse of actors," Pat boomed, so that people at the other tables in the dining-room turned to look at him. "But if a show's a success, the world and his wife will beat a path to the door, no matter what the weather's like. I've played *King Lear* in heatwaves at seaside resorts all over Ireland and people came in their thousands."

"Ah, but that was in the good old days!" Bobby said, having had to listen to such stories all his life, but the look on Pat's face made him add hastily: "I was only joking!"

"Well," Pat snarled, "when Bugsy there has had his little joke, maybe someone will tell me just how bad the house was last night?"

"It was well down in numbers," Maggie said, "but of course on Monday there was a lot of paper, between the critics and the Friends of the Opera House all in on comps., so the box office take was much the same."

"In other words, about a third full," Pat said. "How am I expected to run a company and keep a family on that? I'm in the wrong business. I should have been a farmer, making a fortune out of the EC and then doing the poor mouth to avoid paying tax."

Kate took a large bite of soda bread to

prevent herself from saying anything. Pat was launched on another of his favourite themes, always trotted out when business was bad. The dry weather was worse for Fran's father, she thought, remembering how he had worried about the lack of growth in his grass. He had been so worried about it the previous evening when they got back from the Powder Mills that, in the end, they had decided to say nothing about their plans for the time being.

They had disappeared off to Fran's room and written out the letter on the lines that Kate had suggested, putting it at the very top of a large sheet of paper so as to leave plenty of room for signatures. Then they copied it out again twice, in case they had more signatures than they could get on one or two sheets of paper.

"We'd better get them to write their addresses as well," Fran had said, "to show they live near the Powder Mills, so that the chemical factory will really affect them."

"And take a biro in case any of them say they've nothing to write with," Kate said.

"And a book or something hard to put under the paper so we can ask people we meet on the street," Fran added.

By the time they had thought of everything it was getting late and they agreed that Kate and

Tina would come to the farm as early as they could manage next day. So, as soon as she had finished breakfast, Kate set off for the bus stop. The Ballincollig bus arrived before the one for Macroom, so she decided on impulse to take that, remembering how Fran had said it passed the back gate.

"The nearest stop to the back gate of Carrig Farm, please," she said to the conductor when he came for her fare.

"Top of Inchigaggin Lane," he told her, giving her her change but, when they got there, he stopped the bus right by the gate itself. She remembered then that she had told no-one where she was going. On the other hand, no-one had asked her. Pat and Maggie would surely guess, she thought, that she had gone to the farm again. As for Bobby, he had hardly spoken to her since she had left him standing by the mill gate. In any case, he was the last person she would tell about their plans. He would only tell Joe who might well try to stop them.

She looked in on the calf as she passed the old farm. He licked the hand she stretched out to stroke his head, and stared at her with big round eyes.

"I'll make sure no chemical pollution ever makes *your* eyes run!" she promised him.

When she walked in the kitchen door, Fran and Tim were busy stacking delf from the breakfast table into the dishwasher.

"You're early!" Fran exclaimed, looking at the clock on the mantelpiece, "but I'll be ready in a minute. Only problem is, Tim says he needs his bike today."

"I have to go to Leemount," Tim told her.

"Of course," Kate agreed. "It's your bike. I can go on the bus."

"I was thinking maybe we all should," Fran told her. "The bikes might be a bit of a nuisance going from door to door. There's a bus to Ballincollig from the back gate at 10.20 if Tina only gets here in time."

"Why don't we ring her up and tell her to meet us at the Long Range?" Kate suggested. "It's near as easy for her as sweating all the way up the drive."

"Good idea," Fran said. "Let's ring her now."

So, by 10.30, the two girls passed through the East Gate of the barracks with a carrier bag holding three hard-boiled eggs, a small sliced pan, two biros, three copies of the letter for signing and a cookery book with a hard cover for leaning on. As they came to the bend on the steep hill up which they had pushed their bikes the day before, Fran tapped Kate on the arm.

"This way," she said, "it's a short cut," and she led her straight ahead by a footpath which brought them out at the angle between the two rows of cottages, with the Short Range ahead of them and the Long Range on their left. In front was a large green field with goal posts and a pavilion at the far end, but there was no sign yet of Tina.

"It's bound to take her a while," Fran said. "It's four miles from her place. Let's do the houses down by the Powder Mills first and then we can meet her back here. It won't take long."

When they got near the gate where they had left the boys the day before, they turned left along the houses that backed on to the old mill buildings.

"Let's start at the far end and work back," Kate suggested, so they walked down to the house with the garden gate which faced down the road. Before they had even reached the front porch, a lady appeared in the doorway.

"Is it for charity?" she asked, seeing the paper in their hands.

"Oh no!" Kate told her. "We're not collecting. We just wondered if you would sign our protest letter about the chemical factory that's to be built on the site of the Powder Mills."

"Indeed I will," the lady said, "and so will my

husband. It's a disgrace altogether to think of putting it there. John! John! We need you to sign this bit of paper!"

Her husband came out then, and when he heard what it was all about he said he would be glad to sign.

"I don't know what the County Council were about at all, giving them permission," he told them. "You're great girls altogether to be doing something about it."

His wife invited them inside but Fran explained that they were only just starting and had hundreds of houses to visit. While her husband signed his name and filled in the address for the two of them, the lady ran inside and brought out two glasses of homemade lemonade because, as she said: "It's such a dreadfully thirsty sort of a day."

Kate and Fran were delighted. After they had returned their empty glasses with thanks and gone a small way back down the street, Kate remarked, "If everyone is as nice as that it's going to be a pushover!"

When they reached the gate of the nursing home, they saw three grey-haired old ladies, sitting on white-painted garden seats just inside the gate. These welcomed the girls as if they half-expected them to entertain them with a song-and-dance act or comedy routine, so that it was quite hard to convince them that they had come on important business. When Kate finally managed to explain the reason for their call, the old ladies seemed quite willing to sign the letter, but made a great deal of fuss about doing so.

"Of course I'll sign, dotey!" cried the old lady with her hair in a bun. "Only I have to find my glasses first."

"Surely you don't need your glasses just to write your name?" exclaimed the fat old lady in the blue dress. "I'll write your address for you and show you where to sign."

"But I have to read what it says first!" the old lady with the bun insisted. "Reggie always said I should never sign anything without reading it first."

"I'll read it out to you," said the third old lady, who was tall and gaunt and had her hair in plaits that were curled and pinned up on top of her head.

"I want to read it for myself!" cried the first old lady obstinately. "How am I to know you won't be making it all up?"

"Are you suggesting I'm a liar?" demanded the tall woman angrily.

As the girls looked from one to the other, a

woman in a starched apron came rushing toward them from the house, like a swan defending her cygnets.

"Now, now, ladies!" she cried. "We mustn't get excited, must we? What's going on here?"

Kate had hardly begun her explanations, however, when an angry red flush came into the woman's cheeks and she interrupted her.

"How dare you come in here disturbing my patients like that!" she thundered. "Trying to exploit poor innocent sick people!"

"We weren't doing anything of the kind!" Kate cried indignantly, but the woman interrupted.

"I know your sort," she snapped. "Pestering people to sign documents they don't understand. You have no permission to canvass in here. Now, are you going or do I have to ring for the Gardai?"

Kate realised it was no use arguing.

"Come on," she said to Fran, "we're only wasting time here."

"I don't understand!" they heard the old lady with the bun wailing, as they closed the garden gate behind them.

"I don't think we'd better call next door now," Kate whispered, glancing back nervously. "She's still standing there, watching!"

"We can come back another day, without letting her see us," Fran said. "Let's go and do the Long and Short Ranges."

They had turned on to the road that skirted the sports field and were approaching the pavilion when Kate suddenly shouted: "There's Tina!"

She had swung the bike around the corner before they could catch her, and was turning in the angle between the two rows of cottages before she heard their shouts.

"Hi!" she called. "Where were you?"

"Down at the nursing home, and we didn't get a single signature there in the end," Kate said, telling her what had happened.

"And we didn't even like to call to the rest of the houses with her looking on," Fran added, "so we've only got two signatures from the whole road."

"She doesn't know me," Tina said. "Why don't I finish it for you?"

"Brill!" Kate cried. "She'll be watching out for two girls on foot, not one on a bike."

"Leave it for a while though," Fran said. "Till she's given up doing guard duty. Let's do here first."

So they began where they were. The first house seemed to be empty. It had a desolate, dilapidated look and no-one came to the door when they knocked. At the second house, a very old man appeared and, when Kate explained why they had called, he took the letter in one gnarled, wrinkled hand, which shook a little as he studied it.

"My father worked as a cooper in those mills," he told them. "I remember as a young lad the men leaving the mills of an evening. The very first thing they'd do when they landed outside the gates was to light up their pipes, because of course they weren't allowed smoke inside for fear of explosion, d'you see? They wore timber shoes and leather aprons and the bands my father put around the barrels were made of copper, for safety-like. And whenever the wind blew from the north-west there'd be this grand smell of fresh sawdust from the new sawmills down by the river."

He rambled on and on but, in the end, he signed his name in a scrawly hand and let them go.

"We'll be all day getting a dozen signatures at this rate," Tina said impatiently.

"All the same," Kate pointed out, "he was a nice old man and all that about the mills was very interesting."

"He must have been ninety if he was a day,"

Fran said. "Let's try next door."

"Why don't we each take a page and split up?" Tina suggested. "It would be much quicker."

"That's true," Kate agreed. "You carry on here, Fran, I'll go to the far end of the Short Range and work back towards you, and Tina can finish off the houses down by the mills. The dragon should have forgotten about us by now."

"O.K." Tina said. "Give me a letter."

"If we're finished here by the time you get back," Kate told her as she did so, "you can meet us at the top. We'll go up by the short cut to do the houses up there."

Then, as Tina rode off, Kate gave the last copy of the letter to Fran and set off for the far end of the Short Range. At the very first house, a lovely woman with neat grey hair and glasses came to the door, taking off her apron.

"I'll sign and welcome," she said. "God bless your energy, for you'll have your fill of walking before you're through. My husband's out, but I know he'll want to sign too. What way are you going?"

"Up that way," Kate told her, pointing to the cut.

"Then if he's not too long coming back I'll send him on after you," the woman promised. "And good luck to you!"

She must have brought good luck too, Kate thought, for there was someone at home in every house and they were all willing to sign her letter. Looking across to see how far Fran had got, she noticed idly that the sports field was no longer deserted. There was a lad walking a large dog over by the pavilion. Fran had reached the last house in the Long Range and she herself had only one more in the Short Range to call on. She gave Fran a thumbs-up sign and, five minutes later, they had both got one more signature and were ready to move on.

"Everything's going great now," Kate said, as they set off up the cut. "If Tina's managed to get a few signatures from the houses we missed we'll be well ahead."

Suddenly she stopped dead. Coming towards them was a broad shouldered lad of seventeen or eighteen and in his hand was a big stick.

"You can give me them!" he said, holding out his hand and looking at the letters.

"D'you want to put your name to them?" Kate asked, rather surprised, for he looked very different from the householders they had met so far.

The boy laughed, rather unpleasantly, Kate thought.

"I'm going to tear them up," he said, "and

then I'm going to make sure you remember what's liable to happen you if you're ever stupid enough to try to collect any more. Now, hand them over!"

Kate turned to run back the way they had come. Then she saw the boy with the dog. He was walking purposefully towards them and the expression on his face suggested that his purpose was far from friendly. They were cornered.

6
Stay Wide Awake
or Else Be Caught Sleeping

he dog growled threaten-
ingly and, even more
afraid of him, Kate turn-
ed back to face the lad with the stick. As she did
so, he thrust Fran to one side, pinning her
against the wall with one hand.

"Hang on a minute, Pat. What about the
others?"

It was the owner of the dog speaking. The lad
with the stick hesitated.

"What others?"

"The fellas. He said there were two fellas.
Two fellas and three girls."

"You were look-out, Jer."

"This pair was all I saw."

"And she only talked of two girls on the
phone." He turned his attention to Kate again.
"Come on, hand them over or the Joker might

decide to take a lump or two out of you, and once he gets his teeth into you it's not easy to get him to let go again."

Kate went white, but she thrust the letters into the pocket of her jeans. The lad raised his stick threateningly and the dog growled again.

"Give them to him, Kate!" Fran screamed.

"Your friend's beginning to get the message," the lad said. "Hand them over and we'll only rough you up enough to make it look good."

Suddenly Kate saw Tina on her bike at the top of the cut.

"Tina!" she screamed, "Get the Guards!"

The stick caught her across the shoulder. Then she heard the sound of a man's voice behind them, sharp and authoritative.

"You two are under arrest!"

Kate was suddenly knocked off her feet as boys and dog fled on up the cut. She picked herself up off the ground, expecting to see a man in uniform, but found only a thick-set man with grey hair in a sports jacket.

"Where are the guards?" she asked, dazed, as she put a hand to her shoulder where the stick had caught her.

The man laughed.

"That pair are easy scared. They're from the housing estate over beyond. They've no work and less sense. We've had trouble with them before."

"Are you a detective then?" Kate asked.

"I'm a retired garda sergeant," the man told her, laughing again. "Murphy's my name. My wife sent me after you to sign your protest letter. Just in the nick of time, it seems, but don't worry. That pair are well-known to the gardai for petty thieving and general thuggery. They'll pick them up quick enough."

"Oh, Kate!" Fran gasped. "I thought he'd kill you!"

"I was more afraid the dog would take a piece out of your leg or worse!" Mr Murphy said. "The postman was attending the Regional Hospital for weeks after him."

Tina arrived on the scene then, in a great state of alarm and indignation.

"Are you all right?" she asked. "The shock I had when I saw that lad with his stick raised to you! I won't be the better of it for days!"

"I'm O.K.," Kate reassured her. "My shoulder's a bit sore, that's all."

"You'd better let the wife take a look at it," Mr Murphy suggested. "She was at the nursing before we married."

So they all trooped back to the house at the end of the Short Range and into the little front parlour with the chintz curtains. Mrs Murphy felt Kate's shoulder carefully, moving her arm up and down, backwards and forwards.

"There's nothing broken anyway," she said. "You'll likely have a big bruise tomorrow, but by then the pain should be easing. Something will have to be done about that pair, Michael. They're becoming a menace altogether."

"Aye," her husband said. "I only wanted to be sure this young lady was all right first. I'll slip up to the station now."

"Sit down and rest yourself," Mrs Murphy told Kate after he had gone. "I'll make you a sup of tea. It's the best thing in the world for shock."

Kate said they had to get on with the job of collecting signatures, but Mrs Murphy would not hear of it.

"Time enough when you're rested," she said. "You'll have a bit of dinner with us first."

"We brought hard boiled eggs with us," Fran told her, "thanks all the same."

"And can't you have them with us?" Mrs Murphy said, "and a few spuds and a bit of salad along with them. And maybe a piece of cake after with the sup of tea."

"That would be lovely," Kate said, "but we mustn't stop too long. We have to get loads and loads of signatures or it won't be any use."

"Well now, maybe we may be able to help you there," Mrs Murphy suggested, "for if the three of you are to cover the whole of Ballincollig it will be days before you're through. But I've friends in the town and Michael has more. Why don't you leave me one of your letters and I'll take it to the chapel with me and get everyone to sign it after mass?"

"Oh, would you?" said Fran. "That would be great. We'll make another copy of the letter before we go if you have some paper."

"Here you are!" Mrs Murphy handed her a copy book from the shelf. "You can be doing that while I lay the table and dish up."

"I'll help you," Kate said, following her into the neat little kitchen with its red-check curtains. "What can I do?"

"You can try the spuds with a fork and see are they done yet," Mrs Murphy told her, as she took a cloth and cutlery from the drawer.

"Not quite," Kate said, carefully prodding the potatoes. "Another five minutes. What else can I do?"

"You can tell me how you came to be organising a protest about our Powder Mills. You're not from around here, surely?"

So while she kept a watchful eye on the potatoes and Mrs Murphy set out a clean cloth and delf for five on the little table, Kate told her the whole story.

"So you and your family are staying on Western Road with the mother of the pert little one with the plaits," Mrs Murphy said, "and you're helping her friend from Carrig Farm. Wouldn't it be grand and handy for you now if only the old Muskerry tram was still running?"

When she saw Kate's puzzled expression she laughed.

"The Cork and Muskerry light railway it was called by them that founded it, and it ran along Western Road and out by the Carrigrohane Road. The station was only a step away from where you're staying on an island in the river, where Jury's Hotel is now, and it would have been a great way for the three of you to get to each other's homes if it hadn't closed down when I was about the one age with yourself."

"Oh, I wish it was still running," Kate exclaimed.

"Aye, there's more than you wishes that," Mrs Murphy told her, "for the people living around Carrigrohane never had as good a service since, but there's not so many now remembers it. D'you know, it must be the only train that was ever in collision with a steam roller."

"A steam roller?" Kate echoed, wondering had she heard right.

"Aye!" Mrs Murphy laughed again at the memory of it. "They were repairing Carrigrohane Road at the time and the steamroller was pressing down the loose chippings not far from Carrig Farm. Well, didn't the tram career straight into it and pulverise it, only thanks be to God there was no-one hurt. They had an enquiry over the head of it too, but they never could make out exactly who was to blame, though it was suspected the driver may have had drink taken."

Kate suddenly remembered the potatoes.

"They're done," she said. "Will I take them off?"

"Do," Mrs Murphy told her, "and you can strain them through the yoke there and put a bit of butter on them. And then you can call your friends, for I see himself turning the corner."

When Kate went into the parlour to say the dinner was ready, Fran looked up.

"I was thinking," she said, "those lads must have been sent by someone to get the letters off us, because one of them was expecting Bobby and Joe to be with us."

"Piggy-Eyes!" cried Tina. "He's the only one saw us with them."

"And Piggy-Eyes wouldn't want us collecting signatures against Tenant Blunt," Kate agreed. "But how would he know that's what we were doing?"

"The dragon," Kate told her. "Don't you remember one of the lads saying 'she only talked of two girls on the phone?' The dragon must have phoned Piggy-Eyes and told him we were going round the houses. She thought there was only the two of us because she never saw Tina!"

"And Piggy-Eyes told the lads to get the letters off us and destroy them," Kate said slowly.

"Gave them a few bob to do it, don't you know?" Tina interjected. "Didn't Mr Murphy say they had no work?"

"And told them to frighten us so we'd be scared to start over again," Fran added. "Didn't one of them say if you gave him the letters he'd only rough us up a little just to make it look good?"

"So Piggy-Eyes would know he'd done what he told them and give them the money," Tina explained to Kate, who was looking at them stupidly, as if she had difficulty understanding. "But then," she added as the thought suddenly struck her, "even if the guards arrest those two,

Piggy-Eyes will try something else! Maybe we shouldn't get any more signatures."

"Isn't that the very thing that mean old Piggy-Eyes wanted us to think?" Kate cried. "You can go home if you like. I'm going to get more! And anyway, the dinner's ready!" And she marched out of the room.

"I'm not giving up now," Fran said after a moment. "With the signatures Mrs Murphy gets we could have hundreds and hundreds." And she followed Kate into the kitchen.

"All right so," Tina said sulkily, bringing up the rear, "but we'll want to watch out for Piggy-Eyes."

"And who is Piggy-Eyes?" Mrs Murphy asked, laughing. "He's no glamour boy, by the sound of him!"

"A man who gave out to us yesterday for going inside the gate of the Powder Mills," Kate told her.

"And isn't it a right name to be putting on a man in the Town of the Boar!" Mr Murphy joked, as he washed his hands in the sink.

"Where's that?" Kate asked him.

"Right here," he explained. "Isn't that what Ballincollig means? Baile an Chollaigh, Town of the Boar."

"And that's just what Piggy-Eyes is," Tina

shouted, "a nasty old bore!"

"But everyone else in Ballincollig has been lovely to us," Kate said quickly, "so it can't have been called that because all the people were pigs!"

"Of course not," Fran said. "It was probably because they were famous for pig-breeding."

"Or because, long ago, wild boar were hunted in the woods around here before all the trees were cut down to build ships for the English to fight the Spanish Armada," Mrs Murphy said, laughing. "Sit down and have your bit of dinner while the spuds are hot and forget about Piggy-Eyes."

***

It was a pity that Bobby was not there to hear her. He had flung out of the digs in a really bad mood that morning. He disliked playing to empty houses as much as his father did and, as always when audiences are small, the ill-humour of the management had quickly spread throughout the whole company.

On top of that, Pat had nearly taken the nose off him at breakfast for his badly-timed crack about the good old days and then Kate had gone off somewhere without a word before he had even finished his breakfast. It was not, Bobby thought, that he was mad for her company, but Joe Flynn was going somewhere with his father that morning, leaving Bobby to amuse himself. He suspected Kate was going to the farm again and he had decided that going with her would be more amusing than messing around on his own, even if he had been a bit superior about it when he had had Joe for company.

He decided he would take a stroll out that way and see if Kate were there. She had said the farm was out beyond the County Hall and she had talked so much about it he felt sure he would be able to find it from the many clues she had dropped. So he set out along Western Road and passed the Greyhound Track and the Cross on to the Carrigrohane Road.

Just before he reached the County Hall, he saw a white Range Rover coming towards him. Even as he noticed it, it suddenly turned into the car park of the County Hall ahead of him and he saw then that it too was the commercial version with black lettering on the side panel. He had remarked to Joe the previous day that you didn't see too many of them about and now here was another of them. Or was there? Maybe it was the same one, with Piggy-Eyes at the wheel. Suddenly he felt curious to find out, so he turned into the car park himself, in the wake of the van.

There were no parking places in front of the County Hall and the van continued on around the building. Bobby hurried after it, but when he reached the car park at the back it too seemed full, with no sign of movement or sound of an engine running. He looked around, puzzled. Where had the van gone? It was as if it had disappeared into thin air. Then he noticed that there was a gap on the left leading to a supplementary car park, and he hurried across to it.

There were not many cars parked there but, even if there had been, the white Range Rover would have stood out from the rest. It was sideways on to him, so that he could easily read the lettering and, just as he had suspected, it belonged to the Leeside Construction Company. Even as he read the words, a familiar figure got down from the driver's seat, went around to the rear of the van, raised the back door and took from it a long roll of paper like a plan. Then he slammed the door down and turned towards Bobby.

For a moment Bobby was afraid he had been seen, for Piggy-Eyes was facing directly towards him as he dived for cover behind an old brown Ford Sierra, but he regained his confidence when Piggy-Eyes set off in the direction of the County Hall without another glance in his direction. He passed quite close to where Bobby was crouching, with only the width of the Ford between them, but then he disappeared from view behind the rows of parked cars.

Bobby waited for a few minutes to be on the safe side and then crept cautiously toward the van. He hardly knew why, but the urge to have another look at it drew him like a magnet. He walked all round it, as he had done the day before, but the plywood sheeting was still in place and he was unable to see into the back. Piggy-Eyes must be hiding something really valuable.

Idly he pressed the release button on the back door and, to his surprise, the top half of the back clicked ajar. It was not locked. Without pausing for a second to think, he lifted the top and peered in.

Whatever he had hoped to see, he was disappointed. The inside of the van was almost empty. There was a sack, or something wrapped in sacking, over against the plywood sheeting that screened the driver's seat, and Bobby leaned in, trying to make out what it was.

Suddenly, he felt his legs grabbed and lifted

from beneath him, so that he toppled forward on to his face on the floor of the van. Before he could recover from the surprise and scramble to his feet, he heard the door slammed down behind him with such force that the van shook beneath him and he found himself rolling over against the sacking.

He struggled over to the door, but there was no way of opening it from the inside. He started to bang on it, shouting for help, remembering even as he did so how deserted that section of the car park had been. He heard the driver's door opening and shutting on the other side of the plywood partition and the engine started up. Then he was flung back against the door as the van lurched forward.

He was being taken away as helplessly as a prisoner in a Black Maria and he had walked right into it. Not even a mouse, he thought bitterly, would walk into a trap without cheese, yet here he was caught in a trap that had been baited only by his own curiosity.

7
Here Be Ballincollig's
Old Ruined Castle

hen they got off the Ballincollig bus at the back gate of Carrig Farm that evening, Kate and Fran were in great good humour. They had got all their pages filled with signatures. It was true that they had been run out of several shops by angry people who believed the chemical factory would give a great boost to their business. Still, although a few people had shouted abuse after them, there had been no further incidents. They had been careful to avoid any cul-de-sacs and blind alleys where an enemy might corner them unseen by passers-by and from which there might be no escape.

Walking back to the house, they decided to say nothing to their parents for the time being about the episode with the lads and the dog.

"They'll only make a fuss," Fran said, "and

they might try to stop us from going anywhere on our own again."

As it happened, when they reached the house, they found no-one was likely to ask them about their adventures, for all was bustle and excitement.

"RTE are sending a film crew tomorrow," Mr Mahony told them the minute they arrived. "They're making a programme for *Today Tonight* about Tenant Blunt and our appeal against the planning permission."

"Is that good?" Fran asked, for the mood in the kitchen had changed utterly from one of grim determination to hope.

"It's a great opportunity for us to put our case to the people," Mr Mahony explained. "If we can manage to stir up national opinion, even the politicians might sit up and take notice. They'll be filming here and at the Powder Mills and, if we're to make the most of the chance, there's a lot to be done before tomorrow."

"D'you think you girls could give me a hand with these protest banners?" Fran's mother asked, looking up from the table, where she was painting the words: CHEMICALS KILL CATTLE in large black letters on to a sheet of white paper.

"Of course," they agreed, picking their way

carefully around Tim, who was squatting on the floor using drawing pins to fix another sheet of paper on to a piece of plywood. When Kate peered over his shoulder, she saw that the message on the paper read CHEMICALS CONTAMINATE MILK AND BEEF.

"Can I write whatever I want on my banner?" Fran asked.

"Why not?" her mother replied. "Take a sheet of paper from the pile there."

Kate took one too and found herself a brush from amongst the pile of paints and brushes set out on a piece of newspaper spread out on the draining board of the sink. Fran and her mother were both using black paint, but Kate thought her message should be in green.

"I know what I want to put on my banner," she said. "How d'you spell Carrigrohane?"

And, when Mrs Mahony had spelt it out for her, she carefully painted in big green letters the slogan: KEEP CARRIGROHANE GREEN.

"That's fine," Mrs Mahony told her, "but I wouldn't do any more in green. It won't show up as well as the black."

"What about red?" Kate asked. She felt it would be more interesting if the banners were not all the same colour.

"Red's all right," Mrs Mahony agreed.

"Then I'll do my second one in red!" Kate told her, "because that's the colour for warnings and for stop!"

And she wrote in red paint the words: STOP POLLUTION! TENANT BLUNT OUT! and painted big red exclamation marks after both phrases.

"Let's see yours, Fran!" she said, and Fran held up her piece of paper for Kate to see. On it she had written: NO CHEMICAL FACTORY HERE.

"I did two," Kate said, "so there'll be one for Tina," and she handed them both to Tim to pin on to boards the way he had done his own.

"We're going to need lots more yet," said Mr Mahony, coming into the kitchen just then. "I sent word to Jack to come over with as many people as they can spare and put the word around. Not all of them will have their own banners, so the more we have to distribute the better."

"Will we all be on the telly?" Fran asked him.

"I don't know," he told her. "The girl on the phone said they wanted to do an interview with me, but if there's a big crowd of protesters at the gate they'll surely film them. The more people we have the better. We don't want it to look like a family protest."

He collected up the boards Tim had already drawing-pinned.

"What are you doing with them?" Tim asked.

"You can't hold them up like that," he pointed out. "I'm going to nail bits of wood across them for handles. If we want them to film the banners so they can be read on the television screen, you'll want to be able to hold them up high."

"And hold them still," Mrs Mahony added. "No-one will be able to read them if they're waving around all the time."

"As soon as we have this done," Mr Mahony said, "I'd better take a run into Ballincollig. We're going to need a really big crowd at the gate of the Powder Mills."

"Maybe some of the people who signed our letter would come," Fran suggested.

Mr Mahony stopped in the open doorway, his arms full of protest boards.

"What's that?" he asked.

"We've got the names of loads of people who are against Tenant Blunt," Fran told him. "We got them today in Ballincollig."

Her father put down the boards and held out his hand.

"Give us a look," he said.

As he read down the lines of signatures and addresses he became quite excited.

"Well, aren't you a grand pair of girls," he exclaimed. "How did you think of it at all?"

"It was Kate's idea," Fran admitted. "She thought maybe you could send them to the planning people or something like that."

"I can certainly make some use of them," her father said. "For a start, I can show them to RTE tomorrow."

"And Mrs Murphy's going to get us more," Kate said, delighted everyone seemed so pleased. "But it wasn't just Fran and me. Tina helped too."

"D'you know what?" Mr Mahony said. "I think I'll leave nailing these boards until later. If I went into Ballincollig right away and spoke to one signatory in each of the streets the girls visited today, they could put the word around that we wanted as many people as possible at the gate of the Powder Mills around mid-day."

"Can we come too?" Fran asked.

"I suppose I can't very well say no," her father replied, "seeing it was you got the signatures."

"Well don't stay out all evening," Mrs Mahony said. "I'll have the tea on the table in half an hour."

"Shouldn't take long," her husband assured her. "We can whip round the town and be back here before you know we're gone."

As things turned out, however, it took a great deal longer than he had expected.

***

Bobby had plenty of time to think about his foolishness. The van had driven out of the car park at speed and turned left, but after that it had twisted and turned so much that he had lost all sense of direction. He tried to move the sheets of plywood to attack Piggy-Eyes, but they seemed securely wedged and he reckoned there must be a big stack of them.

After about ten minutes the van stopped and Bobby heard the driver's door open and shut once more, but still no-one came to let him out. Was Piggy-Eyes going to keep him locked in there all day? He began hammering on the door again and beating against the plywood. Then he heard the sound of angry voices from nearby. He could not distinguish the words until a woman's voice carried clearly to him, shrill and indignant.

"Haven't you already brought trouble enough on this house?" she screamed. "Get someone else to do your dirty work!"

Then there was more shouting in a man's voice until suddenly both doors in the front were wrenched open and slammed shut again. Within seconds, the van moved off once more but this time they drove only a short distance before the van began to bounce and rock beneath him so that he knew they had left the road and were travelling along a rough track.

The bouncing and rocking grew worse and worse, until it became so uncomfortable on the floor that Bobby stopped worrying about where he was being taken and became anxious only to get there.

Suddenly, the van gave a final lurch and stopped dead, so that Bobby fell over again. He picked himself up quickly and moved to one side, ready to make a surprise leap out the minute the door was lifted but, when it was, he found himself looking straight into the jaws of a ferocious Rottweiler, with his forepaws up over the bottom half of the door. Behind him was a lad of about sixteen with a stick and, behind him again, was Piggy-Eyes.

"Let me out!" Bobby yelled, but the dog gave a warning growl and Piggy-Eyes laughed.

"You let yourself in," he said. "Didn't I warn you yesterday about trespassing on other people's property?"

"I wasn't trespassing," Bobby began, but Piggy-Eyes interrupted.

"You broke into my van and I could have you charged with attempted robbery."

"I was only looking," Bobby protested.

"A likely story!" Piggy-Eyes jeered. "When I swear in court that I caught you with your head inside the van and tell them the trouble I've had with kids nicking expensive tools, who d'you think they'll believe? You could be in real trouble. On the other hand, if you're prepared to play ball with me and keep your mouth shut afterwards, I just might let you go."

"What d'you want me to do?" Bobby asked sullenly.

"I want to know everything that's going on," Piggy-Eyes told him. "What's planned, who's involved, everything!"

"Involved in what?"

It seemed a perfectly reasonable question to Bobby, but Piggy-Eyes glowered at him.

"Don't think you can play the innocent with me," he snarled. "I know you're in on it. Didn't I see you with the others at the Powder Mills?"

"I don't know what you're talking about," Bobby told him truthfully, but the little piggy eyes narrowed.

"Right! If that's the way you want to play it, you've only yourself to blame. Before the day's out you'll be singing a different tune."

"I'm not playing games," Bobby shouted. "I just don't know what this is all about!"

"Then we'll have to see what we can do to sharpen your memory," Piggy-Eyes said nastily. "Get out!"

Bobby took a cautious step towards the door with one eye on the Rottweiler, but the second he moved the dog growled again.

"Stay, Joker!" ordered the lad, and Piggy-Eyes laughed once more.

"If you don't want him to tear the throat out of you," he said, "I'd advise you to do exactly what you're told. If you force your way into someone's van it's too bad if they happen to have a guard dog in it! Go on, get out slowly. And don't attempt to run!"

Bobby climbed cautiously out past the growling dog and jumped down on to the grass.

"Heel, Joker!" ordered the lad, and the Rottweiler immediately took up a new position beside him, facing Bobby. Afraid to take his eyes off the dog, Bobby could still see that he was standing in the middle of a field, facing a gap between high crumbling stone walls, screened by a clump of old trees and tangled shrubbery. In front of him, the ground became rocky and rose steeply like a mountain track. Perched on top of the steep rocky incline, only yards away, was an old stone castle.

"If I were you, I wouldn't try calling for help," Piggy-Eyes warned him, "not that anyone would hear you out here, but the Joker doesn't like sudden loud noises, does he, Larry?"

The lad he called Larry grinned, but said nothing.

"Right," Piggy-Eyes continued. "Take him to the cellar."

Larry grabbed Bobby by the arm and led him around the base of the rock, the Rottweiler keeping exact pace with him, as close as if he were tied to his ankle. With one eye still on the dog, Bobby made no attempt to resist. At the side of the castle, he saw there was another opening, a floor below the one on top of the rise which appeared to be the entrance.

"In you go!" ordered Piggy-Eyes.

Beyond the opening, Bobby could see nothing but blackness, with only a dim pathway of light immediately in front of him. As soon as he reached the doorway, his body shut out even this and he could see nothing at all.

"It's dark in there!" he protested. "I can't see where I'm going. I could easily break my neck."

"Don't waste time!" The voice was cold and ruthless. "If you don't hurry up the Joker will speed you on your way!"

With this encouragement, Bobby took a hesitant step forward. Then a rough hand gave him a push and he stumbled forward, tripped on a loose stone and fell to his knees scraping his arm against the wall. Piggy-Eyes chuckled nastily.

"I'll be back in a few hours," he said. "I wouldn't try to escape. The Joker will be guarding the door."

Bobby heard footsteps crunching on rock and then silence, followed by door slams and an engine starting. He listened to it grow louder and then die away in the distance. His arm hurt and, as he put his hand to it, it felt sticky. He supposed it was bleeding, but it was too dark to see how badly.

He got to his feet and turned to face the opening. Now he no longer blocked the entrance, he found he could see again. He was in a windowless chamber of which the corners, where the pathway of light from the opening did not reach, were still in darkness.

There was no door to the room and it seemed absurd to remain a prisoner when escape stared him in the face. Maybe Piggy-Eyes had only been bluffing. He crept silently toward the opening, but long before he reached it there was a hideous growling. It had been no bluff. The

Joker was on guard.

He stepped hastily back and sat down, leaning his back against the back wall so that he faced the light. How long, he wondered, did Piggy-Eyes mean to keep him here? His stomach told him it must be lunchtime. Piggy-Eyes had said "a few hours". It was a long time before he had to get ready for the performance, of course, but all the same he was worried. He had no idea where he was or how long it might take him to get to the Opera House when he was finally released.

Now that he could see, he was no longer as scared as he had been, walking into the impenetrable blackness, but it was unnerving that he could still make out nothing beyond the little path of light. He kept glancing into the darkness of the far corner of the chamber, possessed with the feeling that something was lurking there.

Suddenly he saw two pin-pricks of light. Was it his imagination, or could they be eyes, staring at him? No, they were clearer now, staring at him unwaveringly. What could it be, a rat? he grabbed up a handful of loose stones and flung it towards the eyes. With a terrible screech, something clawed its way past him toward the opening. Then he saw it was a cat. He started to laugh at himself for being frightened by a cat but then a ferocious growling from the Joker drove the cat back towards him again.

Bobby ducked as she almost flew over his shoulder. Maybe it was only a cat, he thought, but she was half-wild and completely terrified. She could maul him badly if he did not keep out of her way. Sorry now that he had thrown the stones at her, he drew himself as far away as he could from the dark corner into which she had retreated once again.

I must do nothing to frighten her again, he thought, trying to keep absolutely still, but after a while, he began to get pins and needles in his right foot and had to move it up and down and finally get up and move about. He would have to make friends with the cat.

"Puss, puss, puss," he said uncertainly.

The cat miaowed in reply.

Probably as hungry and worried as I am myself, Bobby thought, and every bit as scared of the Joker. They were comrades in misfortune. He had been stupid to make an enemy of her.

"Poor pussy!" he said, more kindly.

Again the cat miaowed.

Cautiously, Bobby stretched out a hand towards the blackness as he coaxed the cat, but he heard a sudden hiss and withdrew it again just in time as the cat struck out with her claws extended. Just for a second he saw her, back arched and tail waving menacingly, before she drew back into the blackness again.

"Vicious brute," he snapped at her, and then was sorry immediately after. The cat was as scared of him as he had at first been of her. It would take time to win her trust. He began talking to her softly and soothingly. She was, after all, a black cat, and black cats were supposed to be lucky. A plan had begun to form in his head.

***

Mr Mahony had driven first to the Short Range, for Fran had told him on the way there that Mrs Murphy had given them lunch and was obviously the best person to make sure everyone from the Long and Short Ranges turned up at the Powder Mills gate the next day.

"I want to thank you," he said to her, after she had promised to spread the word, "for your kindness to the girls this morning."

"Not at all," she said. "Wouldn't anyone have done the same, after what they'd been through?"

Kate tried frantically to signal to her not to go

on, but Mrs Murphy either did not see or did not understand.

"I'm glad to say the Gardai picked up those two lads," she went on, "for that sort of thuggery has to be put a stop to."

Then of course the whole story came out and Fran had to explain that they had said nothing about the incident so as not to worry her mother.

"Never do that again," her father said severely. "It only makes things worse when you're found out, as you always will be sooner or later. Don't you know the Gardai will probably be calling around wanting you to make statements about it and maybe even give evidence? And wouldn't that be twice the shock to your mother if she knew nothing about it beforehand?"

"As regards the evidence," Mr Murphy told him, "I was an eye-witness to that incident so my evidence may be sufficient. Being a former member of the force may be no harm either, if you follow me, but of course they should have told you what happened. I don't think you need be too concerned about the girleen, for my wife's done a fair bit of nursing in her time and she's satisfied she'll have no worse than a bruise or two to show for it."

"They were lucky you were there to

intervene," Mr Mahony said. "I want you to promise me, girls, there'll be no more collecting of signatures now. You had the idea and got the ball rolling. Now others can carry on from there. Have I your promise?"

The two girls nodded. It had been a tiring day and they were glad enough to rest on their laurels. So, with cries of "See you tomorrow!" they got back into the car to continue their rounds of Ballincollig.

***

Meanwhile, Bobby was starting to put his plan into practice. He had never been known for his patience and Kate, who always complained that he never waited for her, would have been surprised if she could have seen him.

For now that it had finally dawned on him that any attempt at a short cut could prove disastrous, he spent a long time winning the cat's trust. He felt a bit mean about it, knowing what he planned to do, but there was no sign of Piggy-Eyes returning and he had to make his escape and get back to the city in time for the night's performance.

He talked softly to the cat for some time, waiting patiently while she crept closer and closer to him. Even when she was close enough to touch, he waited a long time before very slowly reaching out to stroke her. This time she neither spat or scratched, but he felt her whole body vibrating as she made a low rumbling sound that finally became a recognisable purr. He continued to pet her for what seemed to him like hours, before gently lifting her on to his lap.

"Poor Pussy!" he said softly, feeling like Judas in the Garden of Gethsemane as he bent over to rest his cheek against her fur.

The cat purred louder. Then, still cradling her in his arms, he got to his feet and began to creep cautiously towards the doorway. Remembering how the last time he had done this the Joker had begun to growl before he even reached it, he stayed back a little way and hesitated. The only way this is going to work, he thought, is to take them both by surprise.

It was no use thinking about it. If he were going to do it, it might as well be now. Without warning, he suddenly flung the cat from him as far as he could, so that she hurtled over the Joker's head for some distance before she fell on her feet to the ground.

Then all hell broke loose. The cat screeched in terror and fled as the Joker, all instructions forgotten, gave a terrifying growl and pounded after her in pursuit.

Bobby did not wait to find out who was winning. He had decided beforehand that if he flung her far enough she had a sporting chance of scrambling up a tree or the enclosing castle walls to safety. Now he raced in the opposite direction, stumbling over the rough ground and slipping and sliding down the grassy hill. Once he reached flat ground, he ran for his life, heading for a narrow gap in the hedge bordering the field. He reached it and raced on into the next field along a rough track that he felt sure must lead to a road.

He heard frantic barking behind him and hoped that it meant the Joker was still occupied with the cat and not pursuing him. It sounded, he thought, the way a dog might bark in frustration at a cat up a tree, but he dared not stop to look behind him. He ran on and on, his heart pounding.

He saw a house ahead on his right and thought if he could only reach it he might be safe but, as he got closer, it had a shut up look, as if the owners might be away. Then, gasping for breath, he saw the road. With the last of his strength, he staggered on to it. On the point of collapse, he heard the sound of a car engine. It was getting louder. Thank heaven, help was at hand.

He would be able to find out from the driver the time, where he was and how he would get back to Cork. He might even give him a lift as far as a bus stop. The car was still a little distance away, but he could see it now, slowing as if about to turn on to the side road. He waved frantically at it to try to attract attention before it could turn. Then he noticed how high it stood above the road. It was a white Range Rover.

His hand fell to his side but it was too late. The driver had seen him, for he was coming slowly on towards him. Bobby no longer had the strength to run. He collapsed on to the ditch at the side of the road and waited for Piggy-Eyes to recapture him.

8
There's No Escaping from Family Hassle

r Mahony had driven from the Short Range to the main street of Ballincollig and left word at both ends of the town about the protest. Then he had turned the car in the West Village and started for home, but at Fran's insistence, he stopped the car in the centre of the town so the girls could buy ice-cream, for it was by now a long time since they had eaten their hard-boiled eggs. While they were in the shop, he glanced again at the signatures and addresses.

"Hey!" he called out to the girls as they returned with their cornets, "How did you get this signature? You surely didn't walk all the way to Greenfields, did you?"

"Ah no," Fran told him, "but we got people doing their shopping in the main street and they had come from all over the place."

"Well," Mr Mahony said, "you got one here from Mrs Lucey and that could be interesting, seeing that Mr Lucey works in the County Hall. We might just nip over there before we go home."

He took the turn past the library and the church and turned right again at the factory. He was about to take a left turn about half-a-mile further on when suddenly Kate yelled:

"Look! There on the road! It's Bobby!"

"Who?" Mr Mahony pulled up the car and looked to see where Kate was pointing.

"Kate's brother," Fran told him. "He was with us yesterday at the Powder Mills."

Mr Mahony swung the car back on to the straight and drove the hundred yards or so to where the huddled body lay by the side of the road.

"Bobby!" Kate cried, leaping from the car the minute it stopped. "What happened? And what are you doing here?"

At the sound of her voice, Bobby opened his eyes and grinned weakly.

"I thought you were Piggy-Eyes!" he said. Then he closed his eyes again.

Mr Mahony took one look at his white face and lifted him into the back of the car. Then he turned in a gateway and headed straight back for Carrig Farm.

"What happened, Bobby?" Kate asked again, as the car drove straight on past the old railway station. "And why did you think I was Piggy-Eyes?"

"The car," Bobby told her. "He's got a white Range Rover, same as this."

"Is that what this is?" Kate said, "But Piggy-Eyes has a van. We saw it yesterday, remember?"

"Yeah, a white Range Rover van," Bobby told her, "only you can't tell whether it's a van or not when you see it head on, and I thought Piggy-Eyes was coming back to get me."

"You're not making sense," Kate said. "Start from the beginning."

Bobby struggled to a sitting position. He was beginning to get his colour back now.

"He brought me to some old castle," he explained.

"Must have been Ballincollig Castle," Fran told him. "You were right by the track leading down to it when we saw you. That's real old."

"Fifteenth century," Mr Mahony said, "but it's been a ruin since the Battle of the Boyne. How d'you mean, he brought you? And who's Piggy-Eyes?"

"The building contractor," Fran explained. "Leeside Construction, it said on his van."

"Sounds like Ignatius Quigley, though it's hardly a flattering description. Where does he come into all this?"

"He's working for Tenant Blunt," Kate told him. "He's going to bulldoze the old Powder Mill buildings."

"And he locked me in his van and then kept me a prisoner in the castle," Bobby added. He already looked more like his old self.

"Are you sure you're not exaggerating?" Mr Mahony asked. Clearly he did not believe a word of it. "He's well-known in the neighbourhood."

"Well," Bobby admitted a little shamefacedly. "I suppose I was sort of trespassing."

"That hardly excuses kidnapping," Mr Mahony said, "if that's really what happened, but it sounds highly improbable. For a start, he couldn't lock you up in Ballincollig Castle. There's not a door left in the place."

"There was this dog," Bobby said. "A Rottweiler, who'd take lumps out of you if you moved a step."

"The Joker!" shouted Fran. "That proves those two lads were set on us by Piggy-Eyes."

"You think it was the same dog they had with them this morning?" Mr Mahony still sounded far from convinced. "But Rottweilers are more common around here than white Range Rovers! Besides, Mr Murphy said the guards had picked up those two lads."

"He didn't say they'd lifted the dog though," Kate pointed out. "Maybe he really belongs to Piggy-Eyes."

"I don't think so," Bobby said. "He seemed to belong to a boy called Larry who hardly said a word, but he called the dog Joker all right."

"Then it was the same dog," Kate cried, "but the lads that attacked us were called Pat and Jer."

"I suppose they could all belong to the same family," Mr Mahony agreed reluctantly, "but I find it hard to believe that a reputable building contractor like Ignatius Quigley would lend himself to that class of carry-on."

He was turning into the back gate by the old farm when Bobby suddenly asked: "What's the time?"

"Twenty to seven," Mr Mahony told him. "I'm afraid we're going to be in trouble, Fran, for being so late."

"Maggie will have a fit!" Bobby gasped. "I was supposed to be back by six!"

"Could you possibly drop him back, Mr Mahony?" Kate begged. "I know it's awful to ask when you're already so late, but he has to do the show tonight!"

"I suppose when we're already so late another fifteen minutes won't make much difference," Mr Mahony said, driving straight on down the drive to the front gate instead of turning left for the house.

"Thanks a lot," Bobby said gratefully, as they turned right on to the Carrigrohane Road. "I'm not on until Act Two, but if Pat and Maggie had to leave for the theatre without me they'd be worried sick!"

"They'd let me go on for you," Kate told him, "and maybe they should anyway if you're so tired!"

"I'll be grand by nine," Bobby retorted. "And anyway, you've been missing too. Fat lot of good being an understudy if you're going to be missing at the same time!"

"I'm not your rotten understudy!" Kate snapped, "but if you keep falling down mine-shafts and getting yourself kidnapped you're certainly going to need one—and a minder as well!"

Mr Mahony laughed.

"He doesn't seem to have too much wrong

with him now," he said. "A cup of tea and a rest should work wonders."

"And grub!" Bobby added. "I've had nothing to eat since breakfast and I'm starving.

"That's all you're worried about: stuffing yourself!" Kate shouted. She was annoyed with herself for having been so upset at the sight of him lying in the road.

"Well, now he can do just that!" Mr Mahony pulled up at the gate of Barry's guesthouse. "Out you get!"

"I think I'd better go with him," Kate said uneasily. "Just in case he's not able to go on."

"I tell you I'm fine," Bobby said angrily. The mere mention of Kate taking over his part seemed to have hastened his recovery.

"And mammy's expecting you to tea," Fran protested to Kate.

"I know," Kate said. "Will you tell your mother I'm awfully sorry but I think I'd better stay."

"Don't worry. I'll make your apologies," Mr Mahony said, "but you'll be over tomorrow, won't you?"

"Oh yes, I promise! And Tina too!"

"Good. We need as many as we can get. Maybe your brother might like to come too?"

"Not him!" Kate shouted back, as the car

moved away from the kerbside. "He's on the side of the enemy. We should have let Piggy-Eyes get him! He wants Tenant Blunt to open a chemical factory!"

"What's happening tomorrow then?" Bobby asked, as they walked the few steps to the front door of Barry's Guesthouse, but Kate refused to tell him.

"You might try to sabotage it if you knew," she said. "You and your precious Joe Flynn!"

Bobby turned to say something scathing but, before he could do so, the front door flew open and Maggie confronted him.

"This is a fine time to show up!" she cried. "Pat's raging. He says he'll never cast you in any play of his again as long as he lives!"

"I couldn't help it, Maggie, honestly," Bobby protested. "I was kidnapped by this guy and only just managed to escape."

"You'd better think up a better story than that before you see Pat," she snapped. "You may have a great future ahead of you writing story lines for *Dynasty* but your career as an actor has just become decidedly shaky!"

"It's the truth Maggie, I promise!" Bobby pleaded, but Maggie would not listen to him.

"Just try telling Pat that," she warned, "and you'll be sorry. He's been working himself up for the best part of an hour now, and I don't want to be there when he finally explodes. And as for you," she went on, rounding on Kate, "of course you have to choose precisely the same moment to disappear off somewhere without a word to anyone!"

"Tina knew where I was," Kate protested. "If you'd told her you wanted me she would have given you the phone number of the farm and I'd have come straight back."

"And how was I expected to know that?" Maggie enquired. "You're both utterly irres- ponsible. What did you think we'd do for a stableboy if you were both missing?"

"We were worried about that, Maggie, truly," Kate said. "That's why I came back with Bobby now, when I was supposed to be having tea at the farm."

"Then you could have saved yourself the trouble," Maggie snapped. "We have Bobby now. Apparently you consider we can either have both of you or neither, like a feast or a famine. All I can say is you'd better watch yourselves for the rest of the tour or it will be Aunt Delia for both of you in future!"

"Ah, Maggie!" Bobby moaned.

"And it's no use 'Ah, Maggie-ing' me! Go and get yourself cleaned up this minute. You look awful. And don't delay. Pat's in a mad hurry to get down to the theatre."

"But I've had nothing to eat since breakfast! I'm starving!"

"And whose fault is that? If you'd been here at six you'd have had your tea. There's no time now."

Bobby let out a wail so piteous that Kate felt sorry she had been short with him for she, at least, believed his story.

"If I come too I could run out to the chipper and get something for the both of us," she suggested. "He'll have loads of time to eat before Act Two."

"All right," Maggie said, relenting a little. She took some money from her purse and handed it to Kate. "Here you are, though you don't deserve it. But don't let Pat catch you. Business hasn't picked up so much that we can afford to throw good money after bad and you know how he feels about getting meals out when I've negotiated a rate for tea, bed and breakfast at the digs."

"Thanks, Maggie," Kate said, putting the money into the pocket of her jeans. "I promise I won't buy ice-cream or anything."

"I should hope not. And don't stink the theatre out with chips either. If Pat gets the smell of them there'll be hell to pay!"

Pat had, of course, raged like he did when he played King Lear about ungrateful children and all he'd sacrificed for them, but time was on their side. As it grew nearer to the half he wanted only to get into the mood, costumes and make-up of the blind beggar and he quickly lost interest in Bobby and Kate, who was able to make her trip to the chipper without attracting his attention.

When she got back, Bobby was already in the little upstairs dressing-room at the end of the passage, which he had all to himself, with the figure 8 on the door, under which Bobby had chalked a star, to the amusement of Ned Flynn.

"Thanks, Kate," Bobby cried, grabbing the plastic bag of chicken and chips as if he'd been starving for several days at least. "I forgive you everything for this. You've saved my life. You can have yours here too if you like."

"Big deal!" Kate said sarcastically. "I wasn't going to eat it in No 6 with the extras!"

As they ate, Bobby recovered visibly and Kate felt that it was high time for him to explain himself properly.

"What really happened with Piggy-Eyes?" she asked.

"Like I said," Bobby told her, with his mouth

full. "First he locked me in his van and then he left me all day in Ballincollig Castle, with that monster of a dog sitting outside ready to take lumps out of me if I stirred out. If I hadn't tricked him into chasing a cat, I'd have been there yet!"

"Yes," Kate said, "you told us that. But why?"

"He wanted me to find out things for him—be a sort of a spy, I guess."

"And you refused? Oh, Bobby, I'm really sorry I was horrid to you just now!"

"I didn't refuse! I just didn't know what he was on about. I think maybe I do now though. It's something you and your friends at the farm are up to, isn't it? Something to do with the chemical factory."

"If I tell you, you won't tell Piggy-Eyes, will you?"

"Are you mad? After what he did to me I'd see him in hell first! Mind you, I might have told him earlier if I'd known. I'm not against Tenant Blunt. The factory will give work to Joe's brother and others like him, but Piggy-Eyes is another day's work."

"Then I suppose there's no harm telling you. RTE are sending down a *Today Tonight* team tomorrow to make a film about Tenant Blunt and the objections to it. We're organising a demo outside the farm gates for them to film. I helped make the banners today."

"And Piggy-Eyes thought I was in on it all! Because he saw me with you at the Powder Mills, he believed I was out to sabotage him! I suffered all that today because of your stupid nonsense! I could murder you! I wouldn't mind only I'm dead against what you're doing!"

"You mightn't be if you talked to Mr Mahony," Kate said. "And if you saw the little calf they have. I couldn't bear to think of him choking to death!"

"That's a load of sentimental bosh!" Bobby argued. "Mr Sheridan has sworn there'll be no pollution."

"Of course he has!" Kate was indignant. "What else would he say? It's his job to get the factory built. He's not going to go around telling people things that might turn them against it, is he?"

"You've just taken a scunner against him. Plenty of people believe him."

"Because it suits them! If you'd seen him sucking up to Pat after the first night you'd know what sort he is."

There was a token tap on the door just then and Maggie walked in.

"I thought I told you not to stink the place out

with chips," she said. "I got the smell of them right down the passage!"

"I'm sorry, Maggie..." Kate began, but her mother interrupted.

"And you'll be sorrier when I've finished with you. Mr Sheridan rang me. He said he'd heard that you were involved in some childish protest against the building of his factory. Is that true?"

"Well..." Kate said, but again Maggie cut in.

"I want the truth for once. Are you or are you not helping the people you seem to spend all day with on this farm to organise some sort of demonstration?"

Kate nodded silently.

"Then you're to stop it at once. Mr Sheridan's been a very good friend to us. Only for him the week might have been an even worse financial disaster than it is, and I won't have any child of mine helping to create problems for him. D'you understand?"

Maggie paused, waiting for Kate to speak, but she still said nothing.

"I mean that, Kate," she continued. "Whatever it is that you're doing, don't. And stay away from that farm and those people. D'you hear me? This business could turn quite nasty and I'm not having you involved in it. I want no argument about it. You're to keep away from this demonstration and that's final!"

Then she turned on her heel and left. Kate listened to the sound of her footsteps going along the corridor and down the stairs to her father's dressing-room. A door banged and then there was silence again. She stared at Bobby, stunned. Her world suddenly seemed to be falling apart.

9
Here Be RTE
with Cameras and Trouble

 ate had been unable to sleep. Over and over in her mind ran the things Maggie had said to her in Bobby's dressing-room, like a cassette she was endlessly rewinding and re-playing.

She was no plaster saint, she thought, but she had never openly defied an order as serious and unmistakable as the one Maggie had now given her. She had often been in trouble for dirtying her good clothes or ripping her jeans, for talking too much or interrupting when adults were talking. She had often been punished for giving cheek or for fighting with Bobby and she had often avoided punishment by telling a half-truth or a white lie. She had sometimes even gone so far as to pretend not to have understood what Maggie had meant when she had wanted to do something she really knew quite well was forbidden, but that was impossible now. Maggie had left her no loophole to slip through this time. Her instructions were clear and definite. If Kate went to the farm tomorrow it would be open revolt. It would be what Pat called insubordination!

Yet how could she let Fran and her family down? She thought of the cows, dying of some disease or having to be slaughtered to prevent further infection. Above all, she thought about the calf and pictured him choking to death, the tears streaming from his eyes. Tears came to her own. Why did Pat and Maggie have to side with the enemy?

She pictured Tina, joining the others outside the gates of the farm with her placard, explaining that Kate would not be coming in the end, after all her promises. Suddenly the word "promises" grew bigger and bigger in her mind until she felt that maybe that was the key that would open the door to all she wanted to do.

"I promised Mr Mahony I'd go," she said to herself, "and Maggie never made me promise I wouldn't!"

Wasn't it as bad to break a promise as to be disobedient? And if that was true, whatever she did would be wrong, so she might as well choose which crime to commit! She knew that her reasoning might not impress a teacher and certainly would not impress Maggie, but she pushed that thought away from her.

"I'll go really early before anyone else is up," she decided. "I won't even have breakfast first!"

She would sneak out early and make sure of catching the 7.35. She had told Tina about the demo the previous evening, while Bobby washed the dirt of the castle off his hands and face and Maggie went to tell Pat they had a stableboy for the night's performance, so there would be no need to risk going into the dining-room. To make sure that the sun would wake her early, she slipped out of the bed and drew back the window curtains. A full moon sailed over University College. She got back between the sheets with a great weight lifted from her mind and fell instantly asleep.

As she waited next morning for the bus to stop beside the little blue-and-white gate lodge, she saw the cows going in through the door from the collecting yard. Then she hurried up the drive as if still afraid that Pat or Maggie might see her and call her back.

Fran and Tim were still finishing their breakfast when she tapped on the kitchen door, but no-one seemed in the least surprised to see her so early, for their minds were only on the day ahead.

"There's tea in the pot," Mrs Mahony said over her shoulder and Kate pulled back the empty chair next to Fran, cut herself a doorstep from the big loaf on the bread board and smothered it in fresh creamery butter and honey.

"Will you help Tim clear the table and stack the delf in the dishwasher?" Mrs Mahony asked Kate, when they were finished eating. "And, Fran, I want you to rinse out those things in the bucket there and get them pegged out on the line. We've to get the chores over and done with early this morning, before the RTE people land in on top of us."

They all went to work then and not a minute too soon, for they had barely got the kitchen straightened out when Shep began barking. Then they heard the scrunch of car wheels on the gravel outside.

"They're here!" Tim shouted, running out and around to the front of the house, with Shep at his heels.

Everyone else ran out after him, in time to see Mr Mahony greeting a young woman who had just got out from behind the wheel of the first car. She was followed by a tall, dark girl wearing glasses who carried a clipboard and a stopwatch. As they talked, a second car drew up behind it and Kate could see that the back seat was full of cans of film, while a large black bag and a clapper board lay on the shelf inside the back window.

"I told the others to wait down by the gate lodge until you found out where they could park," the driver of the second car called out to the girl in glasses.

"Right," she said and came over to Mrs Mahony.

"We'll need to keep some of the cars wherever we're working," she explained, "because we have stuff in them, but the rest could be put somewhere out of the way until we move on to Ballincollig. Where would you like us to park them?"

"There's plenty of space behind the old barn near the back gate," Mrs Mahony told her. "They'll be well out of the way there."

"Could you show me where that is?" the girl asked.

"I will!" shouted Tim, "Come on!" and the two of them started off along the drive.

"Hang on, Betty!" the young woman called after them. "I'm going to need you."

"I'm only going to get the cars moved," the

girl said. "They're blocking the drive where they are."

"Can't the boy do it?" the woman asked impatiently.

"Would you mind?" Betty turned to Tim. "Just tell the driver of the first car you come to that you've been sent to show them where they may park and then hop into the car and direct them."

"OK," said Tim and ran off, delighted with himself, followed as usual by Shep. Kate thought the excitement suited him, for he had talked more in the last hour than in all the rest of the time she had known him.

She was amazed at the number of people who finally collected at the house, each of whom seemed to have something they needed to find out, like where they could plug in their equipment, or would it be possible to unplug the fridge during takes because they were picking up the motor on sound.

"But where's the director?" asked Fran in bewilderment, searching amongst the men for one who was not fiddling with a camera or a light stand or a sound boom.

"That's me!" laughed the young woman. "Now, listen everybody! I want to do the interview with Mr Mahony at his desk first, with all the farm accounts spread out around him, then we'll move on down to the farm itself."

"Aren't you going to film the calf?" Kate asked them.

"I didn't know there was a calf," she said, "but it's a good idea. We can certainly include it in the shots at the farm."

"But he's up at the old farm," Fran said, "where the cars are."

"Brilliant!" the woman said sarcastically, but the sound man reassured her.

"It's all right, Jean," he said. "They're tucked in well out of sight behind the barn. You'll be able to get a shot of the calf without moving them."

"Good," she said. "Then let's get the interview in the can. And would the rest of you who are not involved mind staying outside, please? There's not much room and it makes everything much more difficult when everybody's right on top of you!"

"But I want to watch!" Tim protested.

Mr Mahony put a hand on his shoulder and spoke quietly to him for a moment. Then Tim nodded and led the others outside.

"He says we're to get all the banners moved down to the farm gates and be there when the others arrive," he told them. "He was delighted you suggested filming the calf, Kate, because it will give the crowd longer to get over from Leemount. He doesn't want the RTE people filming there till we've got a good size crowd ready for the demo."

So they loaded all the banners into the Range Rover and drove down the drive to the farm gates, just as Tina arrived on her bike and, by the time the RTE people appeared an hour and a half later, they found a sizeable crowd standing outside with banners.

To everyone's disappointment, they took only a few quick shots of the crowd and then went on through the gates to film the cows grazing beside the river bank and the milking parlour itself. With the whole film unit in and out taking shots of the carousel, the bulk tank and the gate from the collecting yard, Mr Mahony was driven almost demented trying to make sure they all dipped their feet in disinfectant but, in the end, he was satisfied, and the dipping process was filmed to emphasize the care that was taken to keep the herd infection-free. In the end, Mr Mahony was satisfied that the pictures would prove beyond all doubt the size, quality and importance of his herd and the danger there would be to them from river-borne effluent coming down from the factory.

As for air-borne pollution, the director assured him that there would be diagrams showing how close the farm was as the crow flies from the site of the proposed factory and the direction of the prevailing winds. Together with all he had said during the interview and the film they would shoot at the powder mills, he could be confident that his story would be put across clearly to the people.

"Everyone will have to think again after that!" he said, as he watched the unit taking a last shot of the river and the sound man recording the peaceful sounds of bird song, water lapping the river and the munching of the cows.

"I hope so," Mrs Mahony replied, "but of course they'll have to give the other side of the story as well. The lighting man was telling me that they plan to spend all day tomorrow interviewing spokesmen for Tenant Blunt and people expecting to get catering and cleaning contracts or work in the factory."

"Then let's hope plenty of fishermen turn up at the Powder Mills," Mr Mahony said, looking worried again. "I put up a notice in the Anglers' Rest and I phoned the secretaries of the Cork Salmon Anglers and the Lee Salmon Anglers."

"And there may be some of the conservation crowd along too," Mrs Mahony reminded him.

"That's true," he said, brightening again. "Jack rang the Green Party and they said they'd be there. I hope to God there's a good turn out. If they get the impression there's no-one but farmers complaining you know how they'll react in Dublin: 'sure you wouldn't mind about them, aren't the farmers always grumbling about something'!"

"But they'll be able to see from all the signatures we collected that it's not only farmers," Fran said. "Didn't you show them in the interview?"

"They didn't film them though," her father said.

"Oh why?" The look of disappointment on the girls' faces made Mr Mahony hasten to reassure them.

"But your efforts weren't wasted. They said the presenter would mention that we got hundreds of signatures, and I can still send them to the Minister for the Environment."

"But they didn't even film the banners properly," Fran said. "And after all the trouble we went to making them. I don't think mine will be in the picture at all."

"I know mine wasn't," Tim added. "They

never shot our side of the crowd at all."

"Then let's make them do it now," Kate said.

Fran looked over to where the film people were heading back toward them across the huge expanse of field.

"They're not going to listen to us," she said.

"They'll shoot anything if we make it look exciting enough," Kate said. "We have to get our banners really high up, so they can't miss seeing them," but her suggestion sounded rather feeble, even to herself. The others were already turning away when Tim spoke abruptly.

"They'll have to drive on up the road to Ballincollig," he said. "Why don't we get up on the wall there and hold the banners out over the road?"

Kate, surprised at the unexpected support, turned to see where he was pointing. Just beyond the second gate into the dairy complex, she now noticed for the first time the remains of an old ruined cottage. Its walls were covered with ivy, but anyone holding up a banner on top of them could hardly fail to attract attention.

"That would be deadly," she shouted in excitement. "Hold my banner, Fran, and give it up to me when I'm ready, will you?"

"Mind yourself," Fran warned. "Those walls

are all crumbling."

"Here!" Tim thrust his banner at his sister too and ran toward the gap into the field. Kate followed him. Struggling with the three banners, Fran squeezed through after them.

There were nettles against the cottage walls, which Kate only noticed when one touched her ankle. It stung a lot and she stopped to turn her socks up over the bottoms of her jeans for protection.

The easiest way to get up on the cottage wall was from the side facing the gable end, where the wall was broken down furthest. Tim scampered up quickly, showering Fran with dislodged masonry as he got from there on to the wall overlooking the road. Kate followed rather more cautiously.

"Hey!" Tim called down. "Pass up the banners before you come up!"

Fran made her way gingerly through the nettles to a point just below where Kate stood on the side wall, clinging to a stone just below the level of Tim's feet. The stone she was clutching was none too steady but, half stooping, Kate turned and took the first banner which Fran held out to her. Then, steadying herself, she straightened, turned back and raised it above her head for Tim to take.

Twice she repeated the process until Tim had all three banners on the top of the wall overlooking the road. Just as Kate was handing him up the last one, the stone to which she had been clinging came away in her hand and she started to topple, only saving herself at the last minute by grabbing the wall with the hand that had held the banner.

"Now how will I get up?" she cried. "That's the stone you used for a foothold."

"Hang on. I'll give you a pull up."

Tim tucked the handles of the banners carefully into the ivy fronts so he no longer had to hold them. Then he reached down and took Kate's hand in his. Somehow, with his help, Kate managed to scramble up beside him on to the wall, though she scraped her right knee painfully on the rough masonry as she did so.

Fran had only scrambled as far as the side wall when, suddenly, Tim let out a shout.

"Hurry up!" he yelled. "They're coming!"

"It's all right. They've still to get the cars down from the barn," Kate reassured him, but then she saw he was right. The director and her assistant were getting into their car, while the cameraman threw the clapper board into the back of his. They were going to go on to the next location without waiting for the others.

"Hurry, Fran!" she called, as Tim struggled to pull the banners clear of the enveloping ivy.

"I can't," Fran called back, "unless one of you gives me a hand. The sticky out stone Tim stood on has gone, remember!"

"There's no time now!" Tim shouted. "They're starting the cars! We must get the banners out!" and, thrusting two of them at Kate, he grabbed a tree with one hand and leaned out as far as he dared over the road to hold out his own.

Kate looked at Fran on the wall below. They would never see a banner held out from there and there was no time to help her up. She would have to get rid of the third banner. Then she had an idea. Digging the toes of both feet in underneath the tough ivy branches that clung to the top of the wall, as if they were straps holding roller skates to her feet, she leaned forward, a banner in each hand.

For a moment, she thought it had all been a waste of time again, for the front car was almost on top of them. Then she saw the director slow to a stop and lean out of the window, pointing to the banners and looking back to the car behind. The cameraman nodded and, as the front car moved on again, he slewed his at an angle across the road, took his camera from the seat beside him and focussed it on the banners.

"They're filming them!" Kate shouted triumphantly to Fran.

Then there was a terrible tearing sound, the ivy branches broke away from the wall, and Kate plunged forward into space.

10
Once There Is Fighting the Trouble's Double

fter the disasters of the previous day, Bobby was glad he had arranged to spend Thursday with Joe Flynn. They had planned to meet as before on the Ballincollig bus so, soon after ten, he set out for the bus stop carrying his bathing togs. A lazy afternoon swimming and fooling around out at the weir would be a big improvement on yesterday, he thought.

He saw Joe waving to him the minute the bus drew up but, when he joined him, he found he was not alone. There were three other lads with him, all older than Joe.

"This is Bobby," Joe said to one of them, who nodded and said, "Hi, I'm Ben and these are pals of mine."

"Where are your togs?" Bobby asked, for

neither Joe nor the others seemed to have even a towel between them.

"No swimming today," Joe told him. "Something came up and we've different sport afoot. You'll see."

Bobby tried to imagine what sort of sport they had in mind, for none of them carried a bag that might have held a football or fishing tackle. Whatever it was, they were not bound for the weir either, for they scrambled off the bus at the earlier stop opposite the East Gate of the barracks.

He followed Joe and the others across the road, through the gate and down the hill. He and Joe had walked up that hill on Tuesday to catch their bus, after inspecting the white Range Rover. It looked as if they were going to the Powder Mills. Then Bobby realised they were not the only ones. There were groups of people ahead of them, all going in the same direction and, when he glanced behind him, he noticed others seemed to be following them. There must be something on, he thought. Maybe there was a match taking place on the sportsground beside the Long Range.

When they reached the corner of the Long Range, however, he saw the crowd were not gathering there. Everyone was going straight on, towards the gate of the Powder Mills, with more people coming up from the Ranges to join them.

"What's up?" he asked Joe, for there seemed to be at least fifty or sixty people already gathered near the gate.

"It's a demo," Joe told him. "Organised by people protesting against Tenant Blunt."

Bobby noticed that a few placards rested against walls and railing.

"But I thought..." he began and then stopped. Kate had said the demo was to be outside the farm gates, but it was better not to tell Joe he knew anything about it.

"I thought," he continued, changing direction in mid-sentence, "that you were for Tenant Blunt. Why are you supporting a demo against them?"

Joe laughed.

"We're not," he said. "That's what they'll all think at first, of course. Then they'll get a surprise!"

Bobby looked at him sharply. He knew now what sort of sport Joe had in mind.

"You're going to break up the demo—is that it?" he asked.

"Sh!" Joe warned. "You don't want to spoil the fun!"

Bobby looked around him uneasily. Maggie had said that things might get nasty. He was glad now that she had forbidden Kate to get involved. All the same, he was unhappy at the turn of events. Mr Mahony and Fran had been kind to him. He could not see them anywhere in the crowd but they must surely be there somewhere. He would hate to end up attacking them, after they had helped him to escape from Piggy-Eyes.

It was at that moment that he saw Larry. He was with a bunch of lads around his own age. Maybe even the Joker was not far away. It was hardly a coincidence. The break-up of the demo had probably been as carefully organised as the demo itself, and the person who had organised it was probably Piggy-Eyes. That was why he had wanted a spy in the enemy camp, so he would know what was being planned. Well, he had learned nothing from Bobby, but he had found out in the end anyway. It was not surprising. It would be impossible to spread the word of the demo to all the protesters without it reaching the ears of friends of Tenant Blunt.

A car came down the hill and slowed at the sight of the crowd, which was growing by the minute. Then it turned on to the road leading to the nursing home and pulled up. A man in a dark, well-cut suit got out and stood for a moment, looking with evident horror at the numbers that had gathered. Bobby had never met him, but he knew at once who he was. He had, after all seen his photo repeatedly in the past few days. It was Gary Sheridan.

As he still stood on the edge of the crowd, hesitating, Bobby made up his mind. Without saying anything to Joe, he fought his way through the crowd and over to the comparative quiet of the side road.

"Mr Sheridan?" he asked.

"Yeah! What d'you want?"

Bobby remembered Kate saying how he had sucked up to Pat. His name at least would mean something.

"I'm Pat Masterson's son," he said.

"Is that so?" Gary Sheridan sounded un-impressed. Clearly he felt this was not the moment for socialising. Bobby knew he must act quickly.

"There's going to be trouble here," he said.

"I guess so. Bloody farmers, stirring up everyone with crazy rumours! I figured if I gave them my word that Tenant Blunt would carry out an Environmental Impact Study, I could get them to pack it in, but I never reckoned on there being this many here!"

"The protesters aren't here to make trouble," Bobby said. "It's the Tenant Blunt supporters."

"Nonsense, boy! You don't know what you're talking about!"

"I do! You're employing Leeside Construction to bulldoze the old mill buildings, aren't you?"

"Who the hell told you that?"

"Never mind. You are, aren't you?"

"Sure. So what?"

"There's a man with little piggy eyes..." What was it Mr Mahony had called him? Bobby thought furiously. Quigley! That was it! "Mr Quigley. He's organised gangs to break up the demo."

"If you think I'll believe a yarn like that you must take me for a real sucker!"

"O K, don't believe me if you don't want to, but when people get hurt it's going to look awful bad for Tenant Blunt, especially if the papers get to know who masterminded the violence."

"God dammit, there's been more trouble since I came to this God-forsaken country than I've ever had in the whole US of A.! Now what am I supposed to do?"

"What you came to do! Speak to the people, only speak to all of them. Say you're having an Environmental Impact Study done so you can give guarantees on safety to the environment, and that you'll be creating loads of employment, provided there's no trouble. But tell them if there's any violence you'll have to think seriously about setting up here. That ought to check the troublemakers!"

Gary Sheridan hesitated.

"There's a hell of a lot of people there!" he said.

"Then ring the guards. Have them standing by in case things get out of hand."

"Now you're talking sense. I'll phone from the nursing home. I know the matron there."

At that moment, Bobby saw a van coming down the hill. Even at that distance, the RTE logo was clearly visible.

"Here come the television crowd," he said.

"God dammit!" Gary Sheridan swore again. "If they film this lot the boss will blow his top. You ring the station while I try and get them to move off!"

He began to elbow his way towards the mill gate. Bobby set off for the nursing home but, before he could run more than a few steps, he saw the police car following the RTE van. He might have guessed, he thought, that RTE would have lined up the gardai for traffic control. The phone call was unnecessary. He turned back just in time to see Gary Sheridan jump up on the wall beside the gate. The crowd fell silent at the sight of him.

"Listen to me, everybody!" he shouted. "I'm Gary Sheridan, Project Manager for Tenant Blunt."

A murmur ran through the crowd.

"And I want no trouble here!" Gary continued, raising his voice still louder.

"Then go back to America!" someone in the crowd shouted, amidst laughter.

"I want to assure you," Gary struggled on, "that there will be no pollution here!"

"That's your story," someone else cut in.

"And we're going to prove it to you!" Gary went on, when he was suddenly hit on the side of the head by a stone, thrown from somewhere in the crowd. He put his hand to his head and fell sideways off the wall into the jostling group.

In an instant, the occupants of the squad car dived in amongst the people, who were now all beginning to push and struggle. It was just the opportunity that Larry, Ben and his friends had been waiting for and Bobby saw Larry seize one of the placards and bring it down on the head of its holder. Then a young garda made a lunge towards him and he, Ben and Joe melted quietly into the crowd. A burly garda emerged from amongst them, holding a young farm worker carrying a NO CHEMICAL FACTORY HERE! banner by the arm.

Bobby felt sick. He had never been against Tenant Blunt, only against Piggy-Eyes and his thugs. He had pushed Gary Sheridan into trying to stop Piggy-Eyes saying there would be no trouble from the protesters. Now one of them had hurt him. There were Larrys and his like on both sides. Maggie had been right. They should all have kept out of it.

He wondered if he ought to go and see if Gary Sheridan was all right. Then he realised the third guard was probably looking after that. Better not to get involved, he decided. He might end up getting blamed for everything. Besides, he was concerned about Fran. If she had been somewhere in that crowd she could have been hurt too. He tried to look for her but it was impossible.

Then he saw Joe and Ben again. Immediately he ducked behind someone before they could see him. He hoped they had not noticed him speaking to Gary Sheridan though if, later on, Gary talked to Piggy-Eyes, they would all know who it was who had told about breaking up the demo.

"Still, I never told their names," he thought.

"It's not like I shopped them to the guards!"

All the same, he had named Piggy-Eyes. His conscience was not troubling him about that, but he was glad they would all be leaving Cork on Sunday. In the meantime, he would have to watch his back. The safest thing to do now was to go straight home.

Beside the RTE van, he passed a man talking to a young woman. "Oh, I got it all right," he said triumphantly. "Rivetting stuff! Couldn't have been better if we'd rehearsed it!"

He sounded pleased with himself, Bobby thought. He doubted if either Gary Sheridan or Mr Mahony would be so pleased. Violence did no good for anyone, he thought, except the TV people who liked to get rivetting stuff for their programmes.

Then he saw a white Range Rover coming towards him down the hill. For a second, he panicked. Then he realised he was making the same mistake he had made the day before. Mr Mahony was at the wheel and there, beside him, was Fran. They saw him at the same time and the car pulled up beside him.

"I'm glad you weren't there!" Bobby cried in relief, as the electrically-generated window slid open. "It was pretty awful. Someone threw a stone at Gary Sheridan and the guards moved in on the crowd and..."

To his surprise, he realised they were not even listening to him.

"Kate's been hurt!" Fran said, and Bobby suddenly noticed that she was crying.

"We went looking for your parents to tell them," Mr Mahony said, "but they weren't at Barrys or at the theatre."

Bobby felt even sicker.

"Is she bad?" he asked.

"She's unconscious," Mr Mahony said. "They've taken her to the Regional Hospital. You'd better get in!"

***

The first thing Kate was conscious of was the smell. She remembered that smell from the times Maggie had cleaned up cut knees after pulling plaster off them. She tried to remember what the stuff in the bottle was called. Something spirit. But the name on the label would not come into her head. Had she cut her knee again? But it was her head that ached. If only it would stop aching, she might be able to get her thoughts together.

She opened her eyes and then shut them again because the light hurt them. Why was everything so white and shiny? The walls of her room had pink wallpaper on them, but then of course she was in Cork. She remembered that now. It must be very late if the sun was so bright and she had to get up early. She remembered that too, though at first she could not remember why. Then it came to her: the demo. She had to get up early so as to get to the farm for the demo before Maggie could stop her. Maggie would be really angry if she caught her. She tried to get up but, for some reason, she felt too tired even to sit up. Then she heard Maggie's voice.

"Kate! Oh, Kate darling, thank God you're all right!"

She sounded more worried than angry, Kate thought. Perhaps she would let her go to the demo after all. Then she remembered. She had gone to the demo and there was something she had to find out.

"Did I fall too soon?" she asked.

"What does she mean: too soon?"

It was Pat's voice. So he was there too! Her own voice had sounded so odd, even to herself, that it was no wonder he had not understood her.

"Don't mumble!" he had always said to her. "I can't have a daughter of mine with bad diction!"

She made a big effort to speak slowly and

distinctly.

"Did I fall too soon? she asked again.

"Before they could get the shot, she means!" Maggie sounded as if she were laughing and crying at the same time. "Oh, she's your daughter all right!"

Kate felt her arm around her, lifting her shoulders just a little and pushing the pillow up under her so that she could see Pat, sitting beside the bed.

"No, darling, you didn't fall too soon. Look!" He was holding out a folded newspaper for her to see, but the big black letters were blurry. She could just make out that it was a picture of a girl on a wall, holding two banners and leaning dangerously forward.

"You got headlines in the *Evening Echo*," he told her.

Kate smiled, and then closed her eyes again, feeling exhausted.

"Just rest," Maggie said. "The doctor said you'd be grand after a good rest. But don't start worrying your head about things. We have to go to the theatre now, but we'll be back tomorrow."

It was only then that Kate really realised where she was. A little while later a nurse bustled up to her with a thermometer and later still she had a few spoonfuls of soup. She had no idea how much later it was, because she kept falling asleep. It was ridiculous to be so tired.

When she woke again, it was to the clatter of breakfast trays, but there was something still bothering her. She tried asking the day nurse when she came round with the thermometer.

"You're not to be worrying your head about such things," she said, popping the thermometer into her mouth, but Kate knew the morning paper must surely say how everything had gone at the Powder Mill gate and whether the people from the angling clubs had turned up, as Mr Mahony had hoped they would do.

"She keeps asking questions," the nurse said to the young doctor when he came on his rounds. He smiled down at Kate and said there mustn't be too much wrong with her so and if she was good she might have ice-cream and jelly for the dinner, but that she must stay where she was and rest for twenty-four hours because she had had concussion. This was all very interesting but it still did not tell her what she wanted to know, so she waited impatiently for Pat and Maggie to arrive.

When they did, Maggie brought roses for her bedside locker. They smelled wonderful, drowning the horrible hospital smell, but it was the little parcel in Pat's hand Kate kept looking at. Pat never gave her presents except for her birthday or at Christmas and she suddenly found she was not too tired to unstick the sticky tape and pull the paper off the little box.

When she opened it all she could do was to cry out, "Oh, Pat!" for there was her own little make-up box with liners in red and brown and blue and green and white and lake, and white powder and a puff and removing cream and sticks of numbers five and nine greasepaint for foundation, just like Pat used himself.

"I suppose you'd rather have had pancake foundation like all the kids seem to use nowadays," Pat said gruffly, but Kate shook her head, which had at least stopped feeling as if it did not quite belong to her.

"This is what I've always wanted," she said, "the very same as you have."

"Well," Maggie told her, "Pat said after Limerick we'd soon have to find a play with a part for you in it, and you can't always be borrowing Bobby's make-up."

Had Pat really said that? He must have thought her understudy performance in Limerick really good if he had. Kate wanted to shout for happiness, but all she said was, "And I'm not letting Bobby borrow mine either!" Then she asked if there was anything about the demo in the *Cork Examiner.*

"Looking for her notices already!" Pat grinned, handing her the paper.

This time she was able to read the headlines over the photo, which read: ACTING TO SAVE CARRIGROHANE.

"They call me an actress!" Kate exclaimed as she read the caption under the photo.

"Because that's what your friend Frances Mahony told them you were," Maggie explained, "fortunately for us."

"Why fortunately?"

"It meant that your father and the show got mentioned too," Maggie explained.

"In both the *Echo* and the *Examiner*," Pat added.

"And, of course, the story was front page news," Maggie cut in.

"So, when we got down to the theatre last night," Pat said, "there were already queues at the box office and, by the time the curtain went up, the house was full!"

"And the telephone's hardly stopped ringing since," Maggie concluded triumphantly. "Bob thinks we'll be booked out for the rest of the week now!"

"That's good," Kate said, going back to the paper for another look. "But it says here there was trouble outside the Powder Mills. Did the demo help stop Tenant Blunt?"

"The less said about that the better," Maggie told her with mock severity. "I seem to remember telling you to keep out of all that!"

But Pat gave her a wink and said: "We'll just have to wait for the outcome of the appeal to find that out, won't we?"

Epilogue

he farmers succeeded in their appeal against the planning permission given to Tenant Blunt, so no chemical factory was ever built on the site of the old Gunpowder Mills at Ballincollig. The site was then resold to Cork County Council, in order that they could extend the Ballincollig Regional Park, which now stretches all the way from Iniscarra Bridge in the west to the restored mills in the east, near to the old millworkers' cottages that are still called the Short Range and the Long Range.

As a result, anybody who likes may now explore the old mills, together with the canal system and sluice gates, or watch James Mahony's cows safely grazing on the river bank at Carrigrohane.

Bugsy Goes to Limerick

by Carolyn Swift

Kate and Bobby Masterson go on a summer
tour with their parents' theatre company and
get involved in an exciting and dangerous
adventure.

POOLBEG

POOLBEG

Robbers on TV

by Carolyn Swift

Maura, Whacker and May find intrigue in the television studios and behind the scenes.

Children's
POOLBEG

The Turf Cutter's Donkey

and

Brogeen Follows the Magic Tune

by Patricia Lynch

"Classics of Irish Children's Literature"

Irish Independent

POOLBEG

A Little Man in England

by Shaun Traynor

The entrancing story of the
adventures shared by Holly, her
family and friends, and an English
leprechaun called George

Children's

POOLBEG

Joe in the Middle

by Tony Hickey

"A deep absorbing story"

Sunday Press

"An exciting and complicated tale,"

Books Ireland

Children's

POOLBEG